# K. ANTHONY WILSON

# Back to You

# Contents

# Author's Note

Back to You is a story about grief, forgiveness, love and friendship. The heart of the story is how we gain, even when we lose. There is always beauty on the other side of pain. When there are clouds and rain, bright sunny days often follow.

This is a clean romance, meaning there is no cursing or details of sexual acts. However, the topic of sex does come up. Please keep this in mind as you journey through the story.

Happy Reading,
  *K. Anthony Wilson*

# Dedication

This books is dedicated to my mother; the one who introduced me to the wonderful world of books and the joys of writing. Look Ma, I did it. I love you; I miss you and I hope I've made you proud.

**One**

## Golden Birthday

Whether you were born on the 1st or the 31st, you have a Golden birthday. Some people call them Grand birthdays or Star birthdays because it's when you turn the age of your birth date. Today is Friday, February 17th and I'm finally seventeen years old. Mama said that since it's the year 2017, it's called a Triple Golden birthday. She's made this a big deal since the day I was born. We even skipped my Sweet Sixteen party so we could celebrate this one.

Tonight is my birthday party and Mama has invited everyone she knows. She's sent about 250 invitations and more than half of them said they were coming. This party has gotten so big that I almost don't want to have it anymore. I just want to chill with my best friends JJ, Jessa, and Xavier.

The red numbers on my alarm clock switch to 5:02. Oh God, why must you keep waking me up this early? My Gram used to tell me that when God wakes you up like this, he's trying to tell you something.

So I lay still, not making a sound. Nothing. If God's talking, I need for him to turn up the volume 'cause all I hear is birds chirping. Gram also told me to seek and I shall find, but right now all I'm trying to find is slumber.

It's still dark outside. There is no light coming from anywhere except for the bright redness of this stupid clock. If there was the smell of coffee wafting into my room, I could understand why I keep waking up so early, but Mama doesn't have coffee until 5:15. That's the time she gets up to read in her reading chair, talk with my dad after his run, or sometimes she'll practice a new recipe for the bakery she works for, *Kate's Cake and Coffee.*

But Mama's not scheduled to work today. She'll only go to the bakery to pick up the cake she made for me. I hadn't been allowed into the bakery because she wanted my cake to be a surprise.

I didn't give her much to go on as far as decorating. I don't like pink or anything girly. My interests include baking—like my mom, reading—like my mom, and skating—not like my mom. My guess is that Mama will design a cake that looks like a book or a roller skate. Or maybe a car 'cause I like cars, too. Whatever she designs I'm sure it will be show-stopping because I have absolute faith in her baking skills.

Looking at the clock again makes me want to throw my pillow, but instead, I use it to cover my head. I shut my eyes and try to conjure up a dream that'll put me back to sleep. Visions of Trevor Watkins pop into my mind. His smooth brown skin, his dark, curly hair, and his one gold tooth on the right side of his mouth. My eyes pop open. I'm not really feelin' that gold tooth. It's not even cute.

There's a light tap on my door. "Come in," I say, removing the pillow from my face.

Mama peeks her head into the room and the nightlight from the hallway shows the silhouette of her petite frame with her hair pulled into a low bun like she wears it at the bakery.

"Happy Birthday, Buttercup?" she says, her voice all chipper.

I don't know how she does it; she's as perky as a cup of coffee every day of the week. With or without caffeine. People in our town affectionately call her "Honey" because she's so sweet, kind, and bubbly.

"Thanks, mama. I keep trying to go back to sleep but I can't."

Mama sits next to me, smelling like cinnamon and vanilla as if she has some sort of secret baker perfume.

Mama rubs my back. "Maybe you're excited about your Golden Birthday party tonight?"

Nah. That can't be it. Mama took it upon herself to invite everyone from our church and other people in my Junior class. Being that she's lived here all of her life, minus the few years we lived in Atlanta, she knows everyone. I don't mind, but I'm not excited. Not enough to keep waking up like this.

"Maybe this means you need to spend more time with me," she says.

I pull the covers back and turn on my bedside lamp. The light shines on her high cheekbones, bringing a smile to her eyes. People tell me I have her smile, but I think they just say that to be nice. When most people see me their expressions show up before their words.

I'm a highly noticeable person and I'm not bragging. All people do is notice me. The first thing they see is this white jagged shape on my left cheek. I have a skin condition called vitiligo. When I was about nine years old, I made the mistake of calling it "Bity Ly Goat," but I know better now. It's Vi-tee-lie-go or depending on who you talk to, it may be Vi-tuh-li-go. Either way, it's a condition where your skin pigment changes.

I'm African American and my brown skin is very brown, but from my knees up to my thighs I'm white. Not like a tanned white, but more like the color of milk. From my face to my knees, I'm a map of the world with white continents and seas of cocoa. The stream of white decreases as it travels up my neck and then takes on the shape of what looks like the continent of Africa on my face.

No one has to tell me I'm hideous. I feel it.

At first, I thought my skin was changing because we moved from Atlanta to Tennessee. I thought maybe there was a change happening in the atmosphere, but that didn't make sense. It only happened to me. Not my parents.

The first day of third grade, dead in the hot heat of August, everyone was wearing uniform shorts but I was wearing pants. Instantly, I made enemies and not friends.

Until I met JJ.

He didn't care what I looked like and befriended me immediately. And then I met Jessa the following year. She has vitiligo too, but hers is slightly less noticeable against her pale skin.

I was the one who got called all kinds of names, pushed in the mud, and laughed at. No one called me by my name. I wasn't Clove anymore, I was Cracked Oreo, Cow, Casper, Ghost Whisperer, and because my dad has become a well-known youth minister throughout the city, I was later called PK, short for Preacher's Kid. Unfortunately, PK stuck and got slurred to "Pink-ay" and later "Pinky." I hate that name, but none of my friends call me that. To them, I'm just Clove. To my parents, well, they sometimes call me Buttercup.

I look at Mama, sitting on my bed. Her skin is all one, smooth, brown color and her smile is so big that it could make the heavens open up. She stops rubbing my back. "I have an idea. How about we make breakfast together? We could do cinnamon rolls or butter croissants?"

Oh gosh, cinnamon rolls take forever. The dough has to rise, you have to make the cinnamon mixture, spread the mixture, roll, cut, then they need to rise again. Followed by making the icing. It's too much. But then, what else am I doing except lying here wondering why I'm awake? Time with mama might be good for me.

I swing my legs over the side of the bed. "Alright mama, just let me put on some pants."

Mama clasps her hands in anticipation. "I'll go get the ingredients ready. We can make 'em extra cinnamon-y the way you like and we can do any type of icing you want."

She is spoiling me, but I absolutely love it. Being an only child has its perks sometimes. I grab her hand before she gets up and she waits.

"Yes?" she smiles.

I hug her. "Thanks, for all that you're doing. I love you."

Mama holds on to me for a while and kisses the top of my head. "Don't mention it. C'mon, let's roll!"

I shake my head at her corny bakery joke.

**Two**

*Star*

JJ always says skating rinks smell like feet and popcorn. He's right. Out of the many times we've been here, that's exactly what it reminds me of as we walk in. We'd come here almost every day for the past couple of weeks so that we could teach JJ to skate, and so Jessa and I could make up skate routines.

My party is 90's themed so Jessa and I both wear our hair in a half-up, half down style. Jessa wears a shimmering iridescent unitard over red tights, with white ankle warmers, a white fanny pack, large bamboo earrings and a purple windbreaker jacket.

I wanted to wear a unitard but my dad wouldn't let me. Instead I have on one of my dad's old Atlanta Braves baseball jerseys over baggy jeans, along with big hoop earrings and all white K-Swiss on my feet. Mama says I look like Janet Jackson from the movie *Poetic Justice*, except I don't have the braids.

I was okay with my look until I saw Jessa in hers. She looks like she stepped straight off of *Saved by the Bell*. She whips her long blonde hair over her shoulders. I try to do the same but my hair doesn't whip like that.

Jessa and I arrive 30 minutes late for a dramatic entrance. My parents, Gram, My Aunt Didi and JJ's mom got here early to set things up. The lights in the rink are dim with swirls of color from a hanging disco ball in the middle of the room. Each table has a rainbow bouquet of tulips in large mason jars. It's a nod to the fact that I was a "Rainbow Baby"; a baby born after a miscarriage.

Tied to the mouth of mason jars are clear balloons with gold confetti swirled inside . The whole scene looks like a fancy box of *Lucky Charms*.

Jessa nudges me. "Dang, girl. Your Mama was not playin' about this party. Everything is glitterin' gold and rainbows."

She's right and I absolutely love it. For as long as I can remember I've always said the rainbow is my favorite color. Jessa tugs on my elbow. "C'mon let's get our skates on."

That's when it hits me that I forgot the most important thing to have at a skating party. "Dang Jess, I forgot the new skates Mama got me."

Jessa gapes at me like I'm crazy and she has every right to. Mama gave me the skates earlier today. They're white with red laces, each wheel has a different color of the rainbow, with the eighth one being pink. I wasn't crazy about the pink, but Mama had them custom made. She even had my name engraved on the outer right side and "Skate Queen" engraved on the outer left.

Jessa clicks her tongue. "Shoot! Now we gotta go all the way back to your house."

"Chill Jess, our neighborhood is like three minutes away. It won't take that long."

Mama briskly walks over to where Jessa and I stand. If she smiled any bigger, she'd be a Cheshire cat.

"Hey Miss Honey," Jessa says to my mom, giving her a hug.

Mama releases her, then steps back to admire her outfit. "You look fabulous!"

Jessa blushes modestly. "Thanks, Miss Honey. You look lovely as well and I love how you and Mrs. Jourdan decorated the place."

Mama expresses her gratitude before telling us to get our skates on so we can enjoy ourselves. But then she searches me with her eyes. "Buttercup, where are your skates?"

I purse my lips together. I don't wanna tell her that I accidentally left them at home. But mama knows me all too well.

Her shoulders fall and so does her smile, but then she plasters it right back on not wanting to show any disappointment. "I'll go get them and will be back in a flash. Go enjoy your party. This is all for you!"

I breathe a sigh of relief, relieved that she's not mad.

"Whaddup, Clove?" a voice I recognize speaks from behind me. *Trevor Watkins.* I didn't know if he was coming because Mama said he didn't RSVP. Trevor's tall, dark and handsome. He's sort of like my friend Xavier except for the handsome part. I can't see Xavier as handsome because he's like a brother to me. And then Xavier has dreads and Trevor has a curly high fade.

"Hey, Trevor," I finally say.

"Thanks for the invite."

"No problem."

Jessa elbows me. "Let's go get some skates."

"Nah, I'll wait for Mama to come back with mine. They'll go better with my outfit." Plus I wanna stay here and talk to Trevor. He looks good in his skinny jeans, crisp white t-shirt, and gold Jesus-piece chain around his neck. It's a nice change from seeing him in the school uniform we have to wear every day.

Jessa pinches my arm.

"Ow!"

She raises her eyebrows letting me know she wants me to come with her so I excuse myself from Trevor and follow Jessa to the skate attendant.

"Why'd you pinch me for?"

"Trevor's trouble," she says. "You need to be careful."

"How do you know he's trouble?"

Jessa tells the attendant she needs a size eight. "I heard things about him."

I'd heard some things too but they weren't necessarily bad, just rumors. And you can't believe everything you hear. For example, I don't believe any of the rumors I've heard about Jessa.

Jessa takes the skates off the counter. "You sure you don't wanna get some skates til your mama comes back?"

I'm positive. Why wear those ugly brown skates when I can wear my own brand new ones? Jessa finishes her laces. "Okay, well. I guess I'mma skate.

See you on the floor in a lil bit."

* * *

It's almost nine o'clock and Mama's still not back. My friends skate over to me. Xavier and Jessa stop but poor JJ keeps rolling. His arms flail in the air before he topples to the ground.

"You alright?" Jessa asks.

JJ puts a thumb in the air, while Xavier helps lift him to his feet.

I glance at the cake table where my dad and Gram are talking to JJ's parents. It shouldn't have taken this long for Mama to get my skates. She's been gone for over half an hour. I know she said this was all for me, but some of this was for her. Therefore, she's missing out on her perfectly planned party.

"Clove, can you please put on some skates so we can at least do our routine? I think the DJ is gonna play our song soon."

I hold up a finger. "Wait a sec." I walk over to my dad and ask if he's talked to Mama.

Lifting up his baseball cap slightly, he scratches his head. He then puts the cap back down and smooths his hand over his goatee. "I've called her but she's not answering her phone."

Gram adjusts my baseball shirt that's fallen off my left shoulder. "Go enjoy yourself, baby and skate with your friends. If she's not back in a few minutes, we'll go ahead and cut the cake."

I'm worried but maybe I shouldn't be. Mama probably just got distracted or something. I ask the attendant for a size ten and sit down to lace the skates up quickly. The song Jessa and I requested begins to play.

We step onto the skate floor and begin skating to the beat. We skate backward, putting one foot over the other. We dance, dropping it down, and picking it back up. I can tell people are slowing down on the floor to watch us. It feels great to be admired for once.

We skate by JJ and Xavier who are talking to some girls from our Church. I try not to pay attention to the way Hannah Hopper is giggling and touching her chest as she talks to JJ. I'm momentarily distracted because I can't help

8

but notice there's something different about JJ. I can't quite put my finger on it but there's something about him that—

The DJ abruptly stops the music and announces that we'll be cutting my cake in exactly five minutes. As Jessa and I skate around, I hear murmurings from people nearby. *Traffic for miles...bad car accident...police and a fire engine.* The word *accident* echoes in my head.

I get off the skate floor and go back to where I last saw my dad, but he isn't here. Gram puts more chips in a bowl.

"Gram, you seen my dad?"

"He'll be right back," She says, tossing the empty chip bag. "He just went to check on somethin.'"

I have a really bad feeling deep in the pit of my stomach. I touch Gram's arm. My hand feels clammy against her skin. "Gram, you don't think that might be Mama in the accident do you?"

Gram reassures me that everything is fine. "Let's cut the cake."

People are already swarming around my cake like fruit flies. It's three-tiered and navy blue with gold stars. The bottom tier is the Pisces constellation. In the middle are clouds. On top is a message that reads, "Always reach for the stars." The cake is simply magnificent and very creative. Mama really outdid herself this time. I can only dream of being like her one day.

The music goes down and the lights dim. Gram lights a sparkler to go on top before beginning to sing the Stevie Wonder birthday song. Soul claps and table drum beats fill the air. It makes me feel all bubbly and warm inside. When the song is over, someone shouts, "Make a wish!"

Although I feel like I'm too old for wishes, I make one anyway. My wish is that I'll always be surrounded and loved by friends and family. I also wish Mama would hurry back. I blow out the sparkler and the lights come back on.

I search around the room for Gram, but she's missing and so is my Aunt Didi. Something is definitely wrong. I can feel it.

Skating away from my cake, I race to the exit but the attendant stops me. "You can't wear your skates outside." Hastily, I unlace them, pull them off, and shove them at the attendant before I run out the door.

Flashing red and blue lights are all around. Police, ambulance, and fire truck horns blare so loud it hurts my ears.

Across the parking lot, I see Gram and Aunt Didi running. I run as fast as I can, passing them as I go.

My heart is racing, bile rises in my throat and I feel like I can't breathe. *No God Please! Please no!* I see the twisted metal of Mama's red car. I reach for the black and yellow police tape but my dad grabs me, lifting me away. I kick and flail against him, demanding that he put me down.

I kick and scream until I feel sick, light-headed and weak. Nausea gets the best of me. Then everything goes dark.

## Three

Two Weeks Later

Day and night pass me by like a train moving rapidly across the tracks.

People are talking to me and I know they're talking because their lips are moving, but I don't hear nothin'. It's as if I'm up in a plane and my ears haven't popped yet. Everything is muffled. Nothing sounds or feels right. It takes a moment for things to register.

"Buttercup, we have to keep going with our lives," my dad told me yesterday. "Your mama would want that. You've missed two weeks of school. It's time to go back."

Why should I ever go back? I was doing fine with reading and taking my own notes. Those were the thoughts inside my head, but I didn't voice them. In fact, I hadn't said anything out loud since the accident.

It's like when Mama left, she took my words with her. I've become a mute; feeling so empty inside. The world around me is still carrying on like things are normal, but I feel stuck. As if I'm waiting on mama to come back; for my eyes to reopen; for me to wake up from a really bad dream.

The only words I've expressed are written down in a furry journal that the Grief Therapist gave me. I don't want no stinkin' journal. How I'm supposed to talk to paper?

"Maybe you can do like *Celie* in *The Color Purple*," Dr. O'dea, my therapist, told me. "You can write letters to God."

So that's what I've done. Every day since I got this journal, I've written the same thing:

*Dear God,*

*I don't like you.*

Or

*Dear God,*

*You make no sense.*

To make matters worse, I'm still waking up at 5 a.m. on the dot. And now my birthday will always be remembered as Mama's death date. It angers me, but I have yet to shed one tear. Not even a drop. Guess I'm still in shock.

Gram touches my shoulder softly. "Clove baby, lemme do something to your hair. It's a mess."

I know it's a mess. I haven't felt like doing much of anything. I've showered and kept up with basic hygiene but I haven't combed my hair in days.

I sit down on the living room floor as Gram sits above me. She pulls and tugs at the kinks in my hair. I don't even wince. Next she puts some coconut smelling cream in my hair and lets it sit for a minute. She begins talking about different things going on in the world, but I'm still reeling over the fact that a drunk driver gets to live after taking out my mama.

I'd heard that the driver was a woman and all she got was a broken leg. A broken leg! I don't know the woman, but I know for sure that I hate her.

Gram stops talking and turns on cartoons. Maybe she thinks the silly antics will lift my spirits. I watch as one character smashes cake into another character's face. It makes me think of all the cakes and delicacies Mama will never make again. No more Tres Leches Cake or fresh baked cinnamon rolls. No more Ginger Molasses cookies that she always bakes for Christmas or Chess Pies for Easter. No more making me sweet treats if I have a bad day.

I remember when I came home from being pushed in the mud by Tisha Manskin. Mama had to take off work to pick me up from school. I cried all the way home. After I showered and came out of my room, Mama had put on her apron and pulled out measuring cups, spoons, flour, sugar, butter, and Seven-Up for us to make a Seven-Up Cake. It was the first cake Mama taught me to make.

"Something sweet makes the heart feel better," Mama used to say.

The box of skates that Mama came back to get are sitting by our media console, all crushed up. Just looking at them makes me sick to my stomach. Had I not forgotten them, none of this would have happened. I will never forgive myself, God, or that crazy drunk lady who drove into Mama.

Gram touches my shoulders to let me know she's done with my hair. Without so much as a glance in the mirror, I grab my backpack. Maybe I look decent, maybe I don't. Who cares?

The front seat of my Dad's 1980 Cadillac Coupe de Ville smells like Mama. But even her lingering scent doesn't bring tears to my eyes.

I look at the clouds in the sky. They're so dense you wouldn't know the sun ever came up. Looks like there might be a tornado today. We've all learned to watch for the signs of a twister. Humid, cloudy days are one of them. Regardless, here I am going to school as if life is normal, as if a twister didn't just come in and wreck my own world, spinning it, tossing it up in the air, then making it all funky and messed up.

What if I have a bad day? Who's gonna bake something sweet for me? Who's gonna tell me that it's okay and that tomorrow is a new day? Who can I talk to?

Dad starts the car. "You ready, Buttercup?"

No, I'm not ready. I will never be ready. I want my mama and I want her now.

In my backpack there's a picture of us at the skating rink when I was five. It was before my vitiligo began. My skin was all brown then. No continent-shaped white patches had taken over my body yet. That came three years later. In the photo, Mama had this really big smile and her hair was in a wash-n-go style with tiny brown coils framing her face. In the picture, I gaze at her adoringly.

I hold the photo tightly in my hand because I feel like I need her with me today. And for now, this is all I have. As Dad drives away from the house, I watch the dark, angry sky. It mimics how I feel.

* * *

My friends wear sympathetic expressions on their faces as they walk towards me in the hall.

I hadn't talked to Jessa, JJ or Xavier since my birthday party. They'd called and texted, but I hadn't responded. I saw them at the funeral but afterwards, I shut myself into my room, not wanting to talk to anyone.

Jessa pulls me into a hug. "You okay?"

I love Jessa like she's my own sister, but what a silly question. No, I'm not okay. I turn towards my locker, trying to recall my combination number. Two turns left 37, three turns right 20, one full turn left 13, push in and pull. Locked.

Hmmm. I was sure that was it.

I try again. Two turns left 37, three turns right 20, one full turn left 13, push in and pull. Still locked.

I'm getting angry. I try once more. Two turns left 37! Three turns right 37! No wait, that's wrong. I have to start over. How do I start over? I yank vigorously on the combination lock. Open! Open! Open! Stupid lock! Stupid locker! Stupid school! Stupid day! Stupid everything! I hate it all!

"Whoa, whoa! Calm down," Xavier says. I glare at him. Does he not see my face? I *am* calm.

Jessa puts a hand on my shoulder. "It's just probably stuck, Clove."

I throw my backpack over my shoulder and walk briskly through the hall to the girl's restroom. I find the handicap stall and slam it closed. Leaning against the door I give myself a mental pep talk. *Get it together. It's just a combination lock.* I feel like crying but no matter how hard I've tried to make tears fall, they won't come. It's like they're still confused about what happened.

"Pinky is back at school today," I hear a girl talking in the bathroom. I don't need to peek through the crack of the stall to know it's Tisha Manskin and her minion Mars.

"Yeah I saw her going bat-blind crazy over her locker just a moment ago," Mars replies.

I look down at my feet and silently wish I had paid more attention to what I wore today. The tennis shoes I have on are caked with mud from when I went hiking with JJ and his family months ago.

Tisha and Mars start giggling. I'm pretty sure they know I'm in here.

"Did you see Trevor yet?" Mars asks. "That boy's got what I need!"

"Well, go get it then, girl. You asking him to the Sadie Hawkins dance?" Tisha says.

I'd forgotten about the traditional Sadie Hawkins dance. It's the only dance underclassmen get because prom is reserved for Seniors only.

"Thinkin' bout it," Mars answers. "Are you gonna ask Jonah?"

*Jonah?* As in my best friend Jonah Jourdan? JJ? Last I checked, JJ wasn't interested in the dance. Neither one of us had ever gone to our school dances in the past. We usually have church events on the same days as the dances and I know my dad schedules those things on purpose. He can be overprotective sometimes.

"I think Pinky has a crush on him," Mars says.

"Pinky has a crush on Jonah?" Tisha asks.

"No, Trevor. Pinky has a crush on Trevor."

How does she know? Have I been that obvious? I haven't even been at school for the past two weeks and before that we had a bunch of snow days.

Tisha clicks her tongue loudly. "Girl, er'body gotta crush on Trevor. But I know for sure he don't like Pinky. I'on care if her mama died or not, she still a cow."

Mars giggles. "That's so mean. Have some sympathy."

The bell rings and the girls hurry out leaving the bathroom completely silent. Eventually, someone will come and check the stalls to make sure no one's trying to ditch or smoke. Sooner or later I'm going to have to come out of the restroom.

I spot Jessa's shoes in front of the stall. "Clove, Xavier got your lock open for you."

She slides the open lock under the stall and it hits my muddy shoe.

"Come out when you're ready, okay? Me, Xave and JJ got you. You'll get through this."

I appreciate her saying that. I have to admit that my friends are pretty great. Jessa has always stood up for me when I didn't have the courage to stand up for myself. She's feisty and as country as a back porch swing; Xavier and JJ are nerds but they're cool and always calm. They balance out me and Jessa.

I close my eyes and hear my mama's voice say, "Procrastination is a thief of time." Taking a deep breath, I open the bathroom stall and mentally prepare myself for the day.

<h1 style="text-align:center">Four</h1>

<h1 style="text-align:center">*Twister*</h1>

I have the last lunch of the day with JJ and Xavier. The three of us sit at a round table near a window. Xavier eats a big bag of chips, a candy bar, and washes it all down with pink lemonade. JJ has his usual vegetarian lunch of fruits and vegetables, and I have a cup of ice. That's all I feel like eating. The mixed smells of the cafeteria make me nauseous. I want to lay my head down, but that might be weird or make other people feel even more sympathetic.

A girl walks by our table, "Hey Pinky, sorry to hear 'bout your mom." She walks away before I can nod a thanks.

JJ extends an apple to me. At first I shake my head, but then I take it, remembering that he once told me apples help with nausea. Part of the random information he gives at least once a day.

Xavier talks with his mouth full of chips. "Yo J, you going to the Sadie Hawkins dance?"

JJ shakes his head. "No, because we leave for the college tour the same night, remember?"

Xavier pops another chip in his mouth. "Oh man I forgot about that. I can't keep up with all the events this year. I think I got senior-itis or something."

I always thought that was a made-up term, but I Googled it and found that it was actually legit. Xavier and Jessa are Seniors so they'll get to go to Prom

17

this year.

"I still don't know why you're not coming on the college tour," JJ says to Xavier. "You might find a school for engineering."

Since my dad is Youth Minister and in charge of the trip, I'm automatically signed up to go, but I don't really feel up to it anymore.

"Haven't I missed the deadline?" Xavier asks. "Even if I could go, I already know what school I'm going to."

JJ pauses before putting a carrot stick in his mouth. "What school is that?"

"School of Xavier."

That's the dumbest thing I've heard but I rest my head on my hand to listen to him explain.

"See, the way I see it is, I make plenty of money fixing people's computers, updating them and making things. What do I need college for? So I can have a bunch of debt?"

Hmmmm, good point.

"I ain't coming from a trust fund like Jessa," Xavier continues. "Me and my mom are out here trying to survive."

JJ begins to explain scholarships, grants, and savings, and Xavier looks at him like he's bored to tears. "*Mane*, I already know about alla dat," Xavier responds.

People in Smalltown and Memphis say *Mane* alot. It's like *homie, dawg,* or *bro*. But JJ has never used the word. He couldn't understand it when he first moved here from France almost nine years ago. He speaks very proper and sometimes mixes in French. The phrase him and his family use most are "*Tu sais?*" (You know?)

The hair tie around JJ's man bun pops unexpectedly. His rich, ginger-colored spirals slowly begin to come down around his freckled face. He's been growing his hair out since ninth grade. And it's grown fast. We have the same curl pattern but I don't think my hair grows nearly as fast as his does. Must be his bi-racial genes.

Xavier takes his dreadlocks out of its ponytail and hands JJ his hair tie. JJ declines, deciding to let his hair hang loose. "You're a Senior," JJ says, pushing his glasses up over his nose. "And you haven't applied anywhere, *tu sais?*

Come on the tour, see some colleges, meet some girls, go to Six Flags..."

Xavier's eyebrows raise at the mention of girls. "I'll think about it," he says and chooses to let his hair hang loose as well. I swear they are always twinning. Their bromance gets on my nerves sometimes. Yet, they both have great hair.

JJ eats another carrot stick."Yep, think about it. We'll be touring a couple of schools with good engineering and math programs."

I find myself staring at JJ, trying to figure out the thing that's different about him. His freckles are still there, his red hair is still thick and coily like mine. He has muscles and that's new but there's something else I can't quite name. Did he get new glasses or something? When he sees me staring, I look away and focus on my cup, turning it upside down to get the last piece of ice to fall. What is it about the last doggone piece of ice that just wants to remain in the cup? I try shaking it loose but it just swirls around the base.

"Inertia," JJ tells me.

What? I don't ask, but I'm sure my face shows the question.

"When the ice stays in the cup. Inertia, an object-"

I get distracted from another one of JJ's scientific facts when people in the lunchroom start clapping, whistling and hollering. It's a time known as Booty Woots. It's a terrible name and game. Whoever came up with it is an idiot. Guys clap when a girl with a big behind gets up to throw away trash or put away a tray.

It's totally sexist. Some guys shout scores: ten for maximum bubble butts, "womp, womp, womp" for small behinds. I'm on the *womp, womps*. They started this at the beginning of the school year but Coach Anthony made them stop, and told them it was "highly inappropriate". Unfortunately, he's not here right now so the ridiculousness carries on.

Tisha and Mars twist their hips super hard when they head to the trash can. People shout *ten* and *nine*. There are some girls confident enough to get up while girls like me stay seated. I have nothing to throw away anyway. And even if I did, I wouldn't dare get up until the end of lunch. Especially not after what happened the first time. I not only got womp, womps but I got "boos" too.

A piece of trash lands in front of me. I don't know where it comes from but I try to search to see who threw it. I can't tell. Turning back around I find that there's a couple more pieces of trash in front of me. Xavier and JJ look around too. Really? Neither of them saw where this trash came from?

JJ takes the trash and throws it elsewhere. Somehow this starts a trash fight. A Snickers wrapper hits me in the face with half the Snicker still in it. I feel the wet, sticky caramel on my face. Gross!

More food hits me and it smells like ranch. A salad? Someone threw a salad at me? Who would do that and why?

Either JJ or Xavier hands me a napkin. I wipe my face just as someone blows a whistle. Coach Anthony barks at the entire lunchroom. "All of you clean this up right now."

There are groans from people and some complain that they didn't even throw anything.

"Jonah and Xavier started it!" someone yells.

This gets Xavier upset. "What!?" he says. "I ain't start nothin'!"

Coach Anthony doesn't want to hear any of it. People start picking up trash. Not me, though. My face resembles a trash can, so I'm not sticking around to clean. I grab my things and walk right past Coach Anthony.

As I run towards the bathroom for the second time today, I pass the glass doors that show a menacing sky. It's so dark the street lights are coming on one by one.

I've forgotten about going to the bathroom and find myself drawn to the brooding storm clouds and the violent sway of the trees. I open the doors. The wind pushes against me but I still my body against it, keeping my eyes to the sky. The mystery of it is compelling.

Drops of cool water land on my forehead. It feels better than good, like small taps awakening me. I should go inside to prevent my hair from getting wet. However, for the first time in weeks, I feel alive again.

Far off in the distance a funnel cloud is forming. JJ once told me that tornadoes in the Southern Hemisphere spiral clockwise. And the opposite direction in the Northern Hemisphere. He would absolutely love to see this. When we were kids, he wanted to be a meteorologist. He has tons of books on weather, astrology, and darn-near anything science-y.

The town warning sirens began to sound but I don't care. I want to get closer. I want to feel something. I wait for fear to pulse through my veins, but still I feel nothing so I keep pressing forward.

Someone calls my name from behind. I pay them no attention because I'm focused on this funnel cloud, the way it twists and gradually gets bigger.

"Clove!"

I wish I was closer so I can see what's inside the eye of the storm, and I wish whoever is screaming my name would stop. Though my feet are heavy, I walk closer.

"Clove! Get back inside!"

I used to think storm chasers were crazy, but I get it now. This sky is amazing.

Arms grab me from behind and carry me away from the storm. I kick so they'll put me down. "Miss Daniels, you must come inside now. It's dangerous."

The last word stays with me. *Dangerous.* It's something that I've never been. I've always been safe, good, and kind even when the world hasn't been that way for me. What's the purpose of being good? What's the point of loving God? Plenty of people do wrong, never go to church and they're still alive to tell their story. I decide right here and now: no more good girl for me. I want to live dangerously.

Five

# Roller Coasters

Last night, Dad hollered at me until he broke down and cried. Dad has never really been the disciplinarian—that was sort of Mama's job. Every now and then Dad would lecture me. Last night I guess he tried to be firm like Mama, but he couldn't do it. At first he was just angry that I had chosen to do something so foolish. He told me I'd put other people's lives in danger because they had to come get me. Then he was concerned and wondered if I should have more sessions with Dr. O'dea. Finally, he covered his face with his hands and left the room, leaving me alone to stare out the window at the perfectly blue sky that was showing no signs of having held a twister hours before.

I sat in Mama's chair and wrapped an afghan around me. It smelled like her. I stayed there for a long time and I don't remember getting in bed; but here I am, staring at the red numbers that light up the darkness again. 5:10 a.m. I want to rip that clock off the wall. I move my nightstand just enough to reach the plug. There! Now it's completely dark.

There's a knock on my door. I know it's Dad. He'll come in after a few seconds anyway. Knocking has always been just a courtesy.

Dad puts my phone on the nightstand. He'd told me he was taking it away as punishment but I guess he's changed his mind.

A small blue light flashes repeatedly letting me know I have messages. I watch the light blink on and off, unsure if I want to know what the messages might say. Eventually I decide to check them.

**Jessa:** *Are you ok?*

**Xavier:** *You're bold.*

**Jessa:** *Clement's house got messed up by the tornado.*

**Xavier:** *I still don't know how you didn't get blown away*

**Jessa:** *R U grounded? Will u be at school tomorrow?*

After I didn't reply back to Jessa she sent another message.

**Jessa:** *That may be a no. Think ur dad will let me come over?*

There's no message from JJ. Not even a missed call. I thought for sure he'd ask me about what I saw.

Dad sits on the chair at my desk. "Buttercup, I'm going to add an extra session with your therapist. I think you need to see her twice a week instead of once a week. I'm also going to talk with your principal. Maybe he can work something out where you can have lunch with Jessa. I think you need as much support from your friends as possible."

Over his shoulder, there's light coming from the hallway. I know Mama's not here, but I keep hoping she'll walk by.

My focus returns to Dad. Jessa doesn't need to miss her class or change her lunch to sit with me. I'll be fine. I throw the covers over my face. Dad waits a few seconds, but eventually I hear him sigh heavily then walk out of my room. I have less than an hour before it's time for school. My phone vibrates.

**JJ:** *Goliath*

Is he calling me Goliath or wanting me to read about David and Goliath?

**JJ:** *Picture loading....*

A picture of a roller coaster appears. Now I'm confused.

**JJ:** *Sorry pic was supposed to come first then title. It's a ride at Six Flags Georgia. Want to ride with me?*

Seems interesting. I've never been on a roller coaster. Six Flags Georgia is the bonus at the end of the upcoming college tour. But I'm not sure Dad is still going to let me attend.

Instead of replying to JJ, I look up all the rides at Six Flags over Georgia and then I start watching various roller coaster videos. Which are the highest, the most dangerous, the fastest? Before I know it, my dad is knocking on my door again telling me it's time for school.

"Buttercup, Jessa's outside."

Jessa? What's she doing here? I don't have time nor do I want to open my mouth to ask questions. I need to get dressed.

After brushing my teeth, and washing my face, I pull on my light blue school uniform shirt and change into some khakis.

"Mornin' sunshine!" Jessa says, greeting me at the front door. I look over her shoulder and notice Xavier and JJ in the backseat of her Honda. Usually JJ rides with Xavier. Why are all of us going to school in one car?

Seeing my face, Jessa explains. "We thought all of us riding together might be a good idea. I drive today and Xavier tomorrow," she says.

Fine. I get in and put on my seatbelt. The boys murmur morning greetings in which I silently lift up a hand, still not ready to speak. I continue watching videos of crazy roller coaster rides. A text message pauses my screen.

**JJ**: *What's your favorite so far?*

I swipe his message away at first but then decide I should reply since he's sitting behind me.

**Me**: *Leviathan in Wonderland, Xscream in Las Vegas.*

**JJ**: *I saw those. Xscream looks fun, you might actually get a chance to ride that one.*

True. There's an eighty percent chance that I'll be living in Las Vegas before the end of the year. That's if my dad decides to go through with starting a church there. Dad calls it "Church Planting." He's been meeting with our Pastor and going to conferences out of town. He's also taken many trips to Las Vegas over the course of a year. Mama had gone with him a few times. But now that she's...gone. I get stuck on the word gone and stare out the window. My phone vibrates again.

**JJ**: *Are you thinking about what it would be like to live in Las Vegas?*

**Me**: *Would you go with me?*

I don't know what makes me ask him that. I don't know why he's the person I've decided to talk to because I hadn't replied to anyone else.

**JJ**: *To Vegas or just on the coaster?*

**Me**: *Both.*

**JJ**: *Coaster yes. Moving again is a question for my parents.*

JJ's family moved here from France when we moved here from Atlanta. Our families are close and we all go to the same church. There have been a couple of people that said they would be willing to move to help my dad start his church. So I can't help but wonder if JJ's family would consider it as well. But JJ has three other siblings, the youngest is his baby sister who just turned one. Moving would be difficult. I don't know what made me ask him if he'd come to Vegas. Perhaps I was only thinking it'd be better if at least one of my friends moved with me.

Maybe my dad won't go through with this anymore. Having a spouse is a big part of starting a church.

We arrive at school and this time I don't even attempt to open my lock. Xavier somehow hacks it open. The four of us have lockers close together but weren't as lucky when it came to our classes. Only JJ and I have a class together.

When I close my locker, I notice the three of them waiting for me. I start walking and so do they. I stop, they stop. I start walking again, they follow behind me. I stop, they stop. Okay, this is weird. I feel like I'm being escorted by bodyguards with backpacks. I pivot towards them and make a face that hopefully displays what I'm thinking.

Xavier says it aloud. "This is weird, huh?"

"Yeah, just a little bit," JJ answers. "Jess, I don't think we need to do this."

Jessa lectures them like a mom, and like I'm not standing here. "Y'all, we said we would do this. Clove needs us."

JJ observes me. Out of all my friends he might be the one who can read me best. Maybe it's because we've known each other the longest or perhaps he's just good at reading body language.

"I think Clove is good. Am I right?" JJ asks me.

I nod.

"See," he confirms with Jessa then looks at his watch. "We need to get going.

See you at lunch, Clove."

Xavier and JJ turn the other way, leaving a frustrated Jessa beside me. "Ugh! Those dweebs. You do need us. All three of us."

She seems like she's the one who needs consoling. I touch her arm. I appreciate the gesture, but the four of us hadn't walked together since middle school. Her class is in the opposite direction. I'll be fine. I start walking and Jessa follows alongside me.

"I noticed you and JJ texting in the car. How did he get you to talk to him when you won't talk to anyone else?"

There's hurt in her voice.

I show her my phone with the messages we sent starting with the roller coaster pic.

"Roller coasters? That's what y'all were talking about?"

I nod. We take a few more steps down the hall, passing people who are hurrying to class. Jessa's going to be late. I don't understand why she's doing this.

"Well," Jessa begins. "I thought you needed all of us, but maybe you just need JJ. I won't walk with you if you don't want me to." She begins to turn around but I catch her wrist.

I don't need her to walk with me, but I recognize that she's trying to be helpful in the only way she knows how. Not to mention, I probably just hurt her feelings. As we near my class, the bell rings. I reach out and give her a hug to let her know that I'm grateful for what she's trying to do. She smiles and I try to smile back.

# Six

# Walk it Out

Each day this week, my friends took turns walking me to class. Wednesday, Xavier walked me. Thursday, JJ walked me. And Friday, was Jessa's turn again. Even though I didn't ask them to walk with me, I felt loved.

None of my teachers called on me to answer questions nor did I volunteer to answer them like I normally would. No one called me "Pinky", well, except for Tisha and Mars.

Today is Sunday and it's cold and wet. Dad and Gram are trying to get me to go to church, but I don't feel like it. It doesn't make sense for me to sit in church, talk about how good God is and how much He loves me, or sing about how I love Him. If God loved me, why'd he take my skin color? Why'd he take my Mama? Why'd he have me be an only child, putting Mama through two miscarriages?

As always, I don't get the option to stay home from church. I'm dragged along for early service, sitting in the back seat with Gram riding shotgun, making small talk about the weather. Once we get there, I sit at a high top table in the Church cafe and drink hot cocoa. As per normal, the flat screen on the wall displays the church service. I can see JJ in the background playing piano and Xavier on the opposite end of the stage playing the drums. My friends are talented. Smart and talented. I've longed to be good at something like them, but I can't sing, hadn't been good at playing an instrument, and I'm definitely not a math or science buff.

"Clove."

I hear a voice behind me and for a second I think it's my mom. But it's JJ's mom. They sound just alike. She kisses both my cheeks as a form of greeting. I do the same.

"Hey Dearest, you know, I'm short a volunteer for Children's church. You think you could help today?"

I could, but I don't want to. JJ's mom has a friendly face and an aura of kindness that's hard to ignore. Her blond-ish-colored sisterlocks are curly and frame her light brown freckled face, making her brown eyes bright and cheery. JJ has her freckles and brown eyes but that's about it. His fair skin tone, and red hair are from his dad's side.

JJ's mom waits for my response. She works in the nursery area. Babies make me nervous because they're all tiny and unpredictable. I like kids, but from a distance. However, Mrs. Jourdan wouldn't be asking if she didn't really need my assistance. I nod that I'll help and toss my half-full cup of hot cocoa in the trash.

Mrs. Jourdan tells me to take off my shoes and wash my hands. As soon as I step through the baby gate, JJ's baby sister crawls to me, her tiny hands use my pants as leverage to stand up. She just turned one on my birthday—or I guess it's *our* birthday. Her one year party was supposed to be the Saturday after mine—if she still had a party.

I pick her up and kiss her little fat jaws. As if Adah senses I need a hug, she lays her head on my shoulder. Though her little body is a fraction of the size of an adult, her tiny hug warms my heart.

But then there are little fingers touching my feet. Another baby uses my leg for leverage to stand up and there's another one behind me. Not gonna lie, this is kinda creepy. It's like they sense my sadness or something and are coming at me like zombies.

"You might want to sit down," Mrs. Jourdan says. "It'll be easier for you to play with them."

I don't want to play with them. I only want to hold little Adah, but I follow her advice. One baby brings me a book to read while Adah stays in my lap and begins to suck her thumb.

Wet fingers touch the white part of my cheek and another little one tries to squeeze into my lap.

This is too much. Don't babies normally gravitate towards happy, friendly people? I'm neither of those today and I definitely don't feel like reading a tiny little book of children's Bible stories.

"*Bonjour, Maman,*" JJ's voice draws my attention away from the kids as he stands in the doorway. "*As-tu besoin de moi?*"

His mom is busy nursing a baby with a bottle. "*Oui. Nous avons beaucoup d'enfants aujourd'hui. Pouvez vous aider?*" she replies.

I only know a little bit of what they're saying. They often speak French at home. I know *Bonjour* is hello, *Maman* means mom, *oui* is yes, and *moi* is me. Other than that, I'm lost. Dad had wanted me to take all Spanish courses so I could help translate for the Spanish-speaking members of the church.

Mrs. Jourdan touches my shoulder. "I'm so sorry Clove, we're being rude. I'm asking Jonah if he can help so that you can leave if you'd like. I didn't expect this many children in the nursery today."

JJ sits on the rug and takes another book from the small shelf. I should leave but I sit still and watch as all the little kids leave me and surround him, including Adah. She's left my lap to climb into his.

He begins to read them a Bible story about Jonah and the whale, but because he knows it by heart, he puts the book down and uses puppets.

The kids watch the puppets, oblivious to the fact that JJ's mouth is moving. Being a ventriloquist isn't one of his many talents, but he does make the story interesting enough to entertain me too. Once the story is over, the kids crawl back to blocks and other toys.

Adah remains curled up in her brother's lap and slowly begins to close her eyes. I'd be sleepy too if I was sitting that close to him. He's got a way of calming people. Maybe it's his voice or the scent of his soap along with that other something I can't quite pinpoint. Whatever it is, it's tranquil. For the longest time, I thought it was his laundry detergent so I'd spent plenty of time in the laundry aisle trying to figure out which it could be. But I think it's just him.

Once again, he catches me staring at him so I avert my eyes. Feeling somewhat awkward, I decide to leave.

I walk back down the hallway and go straight outside into the humid air. Leaning against the brick wall of the church, I watch the cars make *swishing* sounds on the wet street. The scent of rain brings back memories. Mama and I used to hide from humid days like this. We'd go to the bookstore and find a corner to read or share a dessert in the bookstore cafe. It's crazy to think that just a month ago Mama and I were at the bookstore. She was finishing a book by Maya Angelou and I had just started reading *The Princess Bride* by William Goldman for the second time.

I'm jarred away from my memories as people start coming outside talking and laughing. I pretend to be a fly on the wall, watching them lift their umbrellas and listening to them converse about various things.

"You know Jackson is available now," someone says. "How long do you think he'll be mourning his dead wife?"

*How dare they?* Mama's barely been gone a whole month and they're already talking about going after my dad.

"I don't know, you know every man is different," another one says.

I fake a sneeze. The two women try to act nonchalant like they hadn't said anything about my father.

"Clove, aren't you cold? You're going to catch your death out here," one of the women says to me.

Catch death? Did mama catch death? Is that what happened? Did she run right into it? Was the death angel the one who was drunk driving?

Shame-faced, the two women walk briskly to the parking lot.

More people try talking to me.

"Clove, sweetie, it's so good to see you. How are you?"

"Clove, baby girl, how have you been?"

"Oh sweetheart! How are you doing?"

How do they think I'm doing? I put my hoodie over my head. It's rude I know, but I want to be invisible. The interesting thing about not talking is that my ears can hear so much better. The noisiness of people's whispers echo in my thoughts.

"You know they said she ran outside during that tornado," I hear someone whisper.

"I heard she tried to chase it and kill herself."

"She must be suicidal. Hope her father gets her the help she needs. I'm going to make sure he has my card, she should come and see me. I'd be a good therapist for her."

That's Ms. Anita talking. This church has over four thousand members but I know her gossipy voice anywhere. I don't want her help. Anyone who can talk about someone within an earshot of them is more harmful than helpful. I won't be sitting down with her for any sessions.

There's a second service starting in less than fifteen minutes. I start walking across the parking lot and onto a sidewalk lined with trees and flowers. I have no destination, just a need to move away from all the gossipers.

Cars whoosh by me as I walk past a pretty, blooming tree. Taking my phone out, I zoom in on droplets of water that rest on petals. I take a couple of photos and try to see if I can search for the name of the flower.

"That's a Japanese Morning Glory. It's blooming early," JJ's voice says.

He's standing behind me with his hands shoved into his pockets. His hair is tucked into a slouchy gray beanie. A slight breeze picks up and blows a few loose strands of hair in his face.

Finding another flower, I take a picture and show it to him.

He squints through his glasses, then raises them up to see my phone better. "Magnolia tulip," he tells me, while putting his glasses back down.

Turning back around, I take a couple more steps to another flower. This one is a beautiful bright yellow and I know exactly what it is: a Buttercup. Mama's favorite. I take a picture of it as well.

"That's a Narcissus bulb or you probably call it a Buttercup," JJ tells me.

It's where Mama and Dad got my nickname from. It's why I also like the story *The Princess Bride*. The protagonist's name is Buttercup.

"I saw you walking and thought you might want company. But if not, that's cool too and I can head back," JJ says.

I look down the street, then back at him. He nods his head as if that's my answer and takes a step or two backwards, before turning around to walk away.

He's gone too far for me to stop him so I'll have to use my voice. "JJ."

Pivoting on his heels, he puts his hands in his pockets and waits. He's going to make me say it.

"Will…will you…" Though it's a simple question, I struggle with asking it. But I find a way to do so. "Will you walk with me?"

"Yes," he replies.

Just having him here with me makes me feel a little better. We stroll for about five minutes or so until a butterfly crosses our path. It's not a monarch, but it's pretty.

JJ says, "I heard if you whisper 'I love you' to a butterfly it will take your message to heaven."

Is he serious? Of course he's not. But still, I wonder. The butterfly is sitting on the bloom like it's waiting for me, so I tiptoe as cautiously as possible and try to whisper to it. But, where are its ears? This is silly. The butterfly flies away as though it may have been thinking the same thing.

"Maybe we'll find another one," JJ says.

There's a part in the clouds and the sun begins to shine. JJ's eyes are beautiful in this sunlight and he allows me to gaze into them for only a couple of seconds before he shifts them downward. "You uh…would you like to visit your mom?" he asks.

Up ahead of us and to the left is a cemetery. It's where my mama is buried. I hadn't been there yet nor was I planning to go today.

I shake my head no.

He takes a step towards me. "Would you like me to take you to the bookstore later today?"

It's kind of him to ask, but I don't know if I'm ready to visit the bookstore yet.

"Just let me know if you want to go and I'll come get you in my dad's car," he offers.

Over his head a beautiful array of colors arc across the sky. I feel something small release within me though I'm not sure what it is.

JJ twists his body to see what I'm staring at. When he turns back around, the corners of his mouth move upward. "There it is," he says. "I was hoping I would see that again."

Is he talking about the rainbow? He takes another step closer and softly touches my chin. "Not the rainbow. I'm talking about your smile."

Before I can even think of blushing from his touch, he drops his hand. My heart begins to race and my palms feel sweaty. What is happening right now?

Speechless for a completely different reason, I walk back towards the church.

## Seven

# *Read Me*

The aroma of cookies, coffee, and book pages greet me as we walk into the bookstore. The smell is nostalgic and immediately brings about feelings of grief. I stall at the entrance, allowing the cool air to rush into the warm store.

"We can leave if you want. We can try this another day," JJ tells me.

I shake my head. It's a bookstore. No big deal. I think this, but I don't know where to begin. Tea? Books? Share a cookie or brownie with JJ? The cookies and brownies come from the bakery Mama worked for. Who's been baking them now? Do they taste as good?

JJ's hand touches the small of my back, giving me a gentle nudge. I step further inside and the door closes behind us.

He must have noticed me staring at the cafe. "Want something to eat? Or maybe have some tea?"

I don't know what I want to do. I'm getting overwhelmed. My breathing is becoming uneasy so I'm trying to do some breathing exercises like my therapist suggested.

Some people bump into us as they come through the door. JJ puts his hand at the small of my back once again, giving me a small sense of peace and making me calmly exhale.

"It's okay, Clove. Small steps. You made it here, but we can go," he reassures me.

But I don't want to go. I want to persevere. Life has to go on, right? Things keep moving as constant as clouds in the sky. Storms roll in and they roll out. This is what my therapist, Dr. O'dea tells me. I know she thinks I'm not listening to her when we have our sessions, but I am.

Feeling like I need something or someone to hold on to, I grab JJ's hand.

"Geez Clove, your hands are like ice." He takes his other hand and rubs the back of mine. "Let me buy you something warm."

It's not the first time that me and JJ have held hands. But somehow, this feels different. We walk towards the cafe where he orders two chamomile teas. He lets go of my hand to reach for his wallet, but I pull out some wadded up bills and hand it to the cashier. I don't even know how much I've given her.

"You didn't have to pay. I told you I would—" he stops talking because this has been an ongoing battle with us for as long as I can remember; who pays for whom. We sometimes playfully argue about it, but I won't argue with him today. I don't have to because she took my money already. I smile a little and so does he.

JJ hands me the receipt. Playfully, I snatch it from his hand and find us a table.

The bookstore is almost quiet with only the soft sounds of jazz music and low murmurings of talking. There's a distinct familiar voice that I can hear quite clearly. The voice gets louder. "Mars, look. Is that Pinky?"

Great. To my chagrin, Tisha and Mars come over just as JJ sits down with me.

"Hey, Jonah," they both croon his name like it's a love song.

JJ gives them a shy wave before taking off his jacket placing it on the back of the chair. Whoa. How much has he been working out? I avert my eyes before he catches me staring…again.

Tisha notices his physique too. "You've really been working out, huh?" she asks him.

JJ shakes his head. "No, just a little bit here and there." He's being modest. Clearly, there is no "little bit" to his workout regime.

Tisha squeezes his arm. "So, the Sadie Hawkins dance is coming up. Wanna go with me?"

She didn't waste any time. Other than her whisper to call me Pinky, she hadn't even acknowledged my presence. JJ glances at me and I pretend not to listen or care.

"I'm not sure that I'm going."

The barista brings us our teas and a large chocolate chip cookie that smells so good. Tisha and Mars move their heads back and forth from me to JJ. "Hold up! Are y'all on a date? I gotta post this," Mars says going through her phone.

"We're not on a date," JJ says. "Clove used to come here with her mom so I decided to bring her today."

"That's nice," Tisha says. For a second or two we're all quiet. Then Tisha smiles seductively at JJ. "You know, I got a cookie you might like."

My eyebrows shoot all the way up. Why is she so boldly offering him *her* cookie? Especially when I'm sitting here and can hear her. I try to calm down because JJ is not my man. He can date whoever he wants. I should get up and go find a book, but my feet stay put. I wanna know how this plays out.

JJ's cheeks turn pink but he tries to hide it by sipping his tea which is still too hot. I can tell he's burnt his tongue. Mars giggles and walks away but Tisha takes JJ's phone off the table. "Unlock this for me."

He does and she takes the phone, types something, and then puts it right back on the table. "Call me when you know what you wanna do. But make it quick because I have other people to consider."

JJ scrutinizes the numbers she put in his phone. "Okay, um, I'll make sure to take that into consideration."

When Tisha finally walks away, I'm relieved. She's so rude and arrogant. I break off a piece of the chocolate chip cookie and taste it. It's not my mama's but it's still good.

JJ nudges the plate closer to me. I nudge it back. He gives me a smirk like he knows I'm going to want more. He's right, I do want more. I hadn't had one of these in a long time.

Because our table is small, I accidentally step on his foot. "Sorry," I say.

This is the second time I've spoken since the accident and I've noticed that I've only spoken to *him*.

He doesn't bother to move his foot so neither do I. The heat from his leg warms me up better than the tea. After a minute or two of silence, JJ brings up the spring break college tour and how we'll have a free day to hang out in downtown Atlanta. Our Spring break begins on Thursday after school, so we'll leave late Thursday night, tour colleges Friday and Saturday, then have Saturday afternoon and evening to explore. Sunday will be our trip to Six Flags. JJ tells me he wants to go to the Georgia Aquarium during our free time because it's the largest aquarium in the Western Hemisphere. I just let him talk. He usually doesn't talk this much unless it's about something nerdy like science.

I pinch another piece of the cookie. By now it's practically gone. I've barely left him a fourth. So once again, he slowly pushes the plate over to my side

"Just take the rest of it," he says. "I'm not going to eat it."

Semi-jokingly, I say, "You want Tisha's cookie. Is that why you don't want this one?"

JJ shakes his head and takes the top off his tea to let it cool faster. "Nope. I think she may be shy of a few chocolate chips. Look…" He turns his phone towards me. Not including the area code, Tisha only put in six numbers.

I cover my chuckle. I knew he wasn't interested in her, but I had to hear him say it to be certain.

Once, Tisha and I were lab partners and she lit her eyebrows on fire while messing with the Bunsen burner. After that she started drawing on her eyebrows. Problem was she couldn't really draw that well. Her eyebrows were too high. For three days, she had one facial expression.

"Do you think you might ask Trevor to the dance?" JJ asks.

I knit my eyebrows together. Why on Earth would I do that? Or better yet why does he think I would? I take the top off of my tea to blow it.

"You like him, right? I heard you tell Jessa that you did and it kind of seems like you do."

I didn't realize he'd heard me and Jessa talking about Trevor. But now that I think about it, he probably hears a lot because he doesn't talk much, kind of like what I've been doing. He's only talking as much as he is now out of desperation to get me to say something. I shrug my shoulders and direct my attention towards the aisle of clearance books.

JJ takes another sip of his tea and gets up to throw away the leftover cookie. Quickly, I reach out and grab it before he throws it away.

JJ smirks. "You are so predictable."

There's melted chocolate on my fingers and I reach for his face to wipe it on his cheek but he dodges me.

"See," he smiles. "Predictable."

# Eight

## *Versus Verses*

I have to make-up a Chemistry test after school. I get the privilege of being in here with Trevor because I'd heard he was out with the flu last week. I finish my test in less than nine minutes. Mr. G wants me to stay until he's done grading so I do some other homework while I wait.

Trevor returns his paper shortly after I hand in mine. He's wearing a burgundy sweater over a white button-up that neatly covers his khaki pants. I have on the same uniform: burgundy sweater and white collar shirt but instead of khaki pants, I wear a plaid knee-length skirt with knit tights.

Trevor brushes up against my leg when he walks by. We had to have a desk between us while we took the test, but now that it's over, Trevor sits behind me. He smells earthy, like patchouli and something spicy. He taps me on my right shoulder then hands me a folded note. Even though Mr. G isn't paying us any attention, I try making as little noise as possible when I open it.

*You were a total baddie for walking outside last Monday. I heard about it.*

I guess that was a compliment so I write *Thanks* and pass the note back to him. The note lands back over my shoulder.

*What are u doing after this?*

Jessa's waiting to take me home so basically my plans consist of homework and maybe a nap.

I write *Homework* and pass it back.

It returns to my desk.

*Think you can go somewhere with me?*

Is Trevor asking me out? No. He's just asking me to go somewhere with him.

*Where?*

*Come with me and find out.*

I can't go with him. Or can I? It's not like I have anything else going on at home. And I'm pretty sure Dad is where he always is, having a meeting with the church about his church for Las Vegas.

*Ok,* I write back. I'm starting to feel exhilarated like I did last week when I walked into the storm.

We get our tests back. No surprise that I've passed with a 98 percent. Mr. G's tests are always easy. You'd have to be a moron not to pass. Trevor holds the door open for me as we walk out the building. *Chivalrous. Nice.* I make a mental check mark on my list of qualifications.

I follow him to his Chevy Impala. It has to be a 1988 or '89. It's clean too; chrome wheels and a new coat of candy blue paint. I'm into cars, one of the perks of being an only child with a father who's a car lover. I even took a shop class last semester.

"What time do you have to be home?" Trevor asks once we're in the car. "I know your dad got you on lock and key."

I shrug like it's not a concern.

Trevor backs out of the parking space. "Still not talking, huh? How do we communicate if you ain't gon' talk to me?"

He can't read my mind like JJ? He misses a point. Just kidding. No one's a mind reader. It's unfair for me to compare him to JJ.

Trevor reaches across me, "Scuse me," he says as he quickly pulls out a bag of cough drops. He's quick, but not quick enough. Shiny, condom wrappers catch my eye.

"Sorry," Trevor says. "I still got a little bit of a cold, but I don't think I'll get you sick. You want one?"

I don't have a cold. Why do I need a cough drop? Trevor tells me why.

"You haven't been talking so there's less air going into your mouth. Your breath is probably on hum status right now."

Oh wow. He just slick tried to tell me my breath stinks. He laughs and I notice his pretty white teeth and the one gold tooth. I'll give him a bonus mark for brushing and flossing, but that gold, ummm…it's got to go. Trevor might be right about the breath thing. I hold my palm open for the cough drop. He tilts the bag and all the cough drops spill into my hand, with some falling on the floor.

Dang! I don't need that many. My breath isn't *that* bad.

"Whoops. Just take what you want. I'll pick the rest up later," Trevor says.

I admire the leather seats he has in front. He's left it as a bench instead of replacing it with bucket seats. The back of the car looks even better, plush and cozy.

"Your ol' man got one a dese cars, don't he?" Trevor asks.

I chew on the side of my cheek as I recall what JJ said about people talking as though words start with "d's".

If Trevor is referring to my dad having a classic car, the answer to his question is yes. If he's asking if my dad has an Impala, the answer is no. So I shake my head no.

"Gotta keep my eyes on the road sweetheart. Can't see ya moving ya head as a response," Trevor tells me.

Then how did he know I just responded?

"Do you listen to rap music?" he asks.

I nod again. He can see me. I know he can. At a stop light, Trevor uses his phone to turn on a song.

There's talking at the intro and then the beat drops. I've heard this on the radio before so I start bobbing my head to the beat.

Trevor starts grinning. "Okay, I see you, girl. So you do know good music when you hear it. And you got rhythm. "

Of course I have rhythm. Didn't he see me at the skating rink?

The guy on the song starts rapping and it's full out cursing for the first three stanzas. I stop bopping my head.

"Too much cursing for you?"Although Trevor asks, he doesn't turn the music off nor decrease the volume. I don't wanna seem uncool so I shake my head no. Finally he turns the music down, for which I'm grateful. It was starting to get a little uncomfortable.

"You know, Clove, I'on know how this gon' work out if you not gon' talk to me. Relationships take communication."

Who says I want to be in a relationship with him? And *I am* communicating, just maybe not in the way he wants me to. JJ would know exactly—wait. I have to stop comparing Trevor to JJ. I don't even know why I'm doing it.

Jessa texts me. *Are you still taking a test?*

Oh shoot! I forgot to tell Jess I left with Trevor.

**Me**: *I left already.*

**Jessa**: *What?! With who? How long ago?*

**Me**: *Trevor. 3 min.*

**Jessa**: *Wow*

She's upset. I can tell from only those three letters. What I can't tell is if she's more upset about me leaving without telling her or that I left with Trevor. Just as I'm texting an apology, she texts back.

**Jessa**: *Be careful. He's tricky.*

How would she know? Something must have gone down between the two of them and I need to find out what.

Trevor is driving south of Smalltown towards a neighboring town that's still a part of the city. I wanna know where we're going but I'll find out soon enough. I'm not gonna waste my fresh cough drop breath on that question.

"So….do you and JJ go out together often? Heard y'all was at the bookstore sharing tea and crumpets and stuff. You asking him to the Sadie Hawkins dance?"

I was going to shake my head no but that answer doesn't cover both of the questions he asked me.

"We're just friends. No."

"So she speaks," Trevor says, nodding slowly. "Are you saying no that you're not going to the Sadie Hawkins dance or no you and JJ don't go out together often? I mean having coffee and sharing a cookie together seems like a date to me."

Mars has a big mouth. "It was cold out so we had tea. We're just friends and no, we're not going to the dance together."

"You sure? He's kinda…" Trevor pauses as though he's thinking carefully. "Protective. Yeah that's the word. He's protective of you and so is Xavier. You don't like either one of them?"

"No."

"No you're not sure? Or no, you don't like them?"

If he'd quit asking me two questions at once, this wouldn't be so confusing. This is my time to be clear and use my voice so things don't get misconstrued. "We're all just friends."

I'm ready for this game of twenty-one questions to be over but I guess I'm not being fair. If he wants to get to know me, then I should put in a little more effort. "I don't think I'm going to the dance."

We stop at a traffic light and Trevor puts his arm on the back of my seat. His hand slowly sweeps my hair off my neck, giving me a small sensation inside.

"Why not?" he asks.

That's a good question. We leave for the college tour at midnight, I'll have plenty of time to go to the dance. Still, I need to get to know Trevor more before I ask him to go with me.

He pulls into a parking space in front of a tattoo and piercing shop. Alarms are sounding in my head but I turn them off because I chose to go with Trevor as a part of having adventure and being dangerous for once.

Trevor opens my car door as well as the door to the parlor. "My lady," he says and bows. A bell chimes as we walk in and I'm greeted by the smell of incense and sterile alcohol. Jazz plays in the background: *Mystic Brew* by Ronnie Foster. I only recognize it because Xavier and JJ listen to him sometimes.

On the walls of the shop, rules are posted along with tattoo art and seductive photos of tattooed women. A girl with pink hair and a bunch of piercings on her face sits on a stool behind the cash register, reading a book and blowing a wad of purple bubble gum.

A short, stocky guy with a snapback cap and a long black beard gets up when he sees us.

Trevor gives the guy a handshake that turns into a one-armed hug. "What up, Unc?"

"What up, nephew!" The guy says. Trevor introduces me to whom I assume is his uncle. "This is Clove. She's here to watch me get my new tatt."

My eyes open real wide. That's why he brought me here? I thought you had to have a parent present to get a tattoo.

"Dis my Uncle Kinsey," Trevor says to me. "He's my legal guardian."

I had no idea Trevor lived with his Uncle.

Kinsey extends his hand and I shake it nervously, while wondering what happened to Trevor's parents.

Kinsey looks at Trevor. "Does she talk?"

Trevor explains, "She goin' through some thangs but I'mma get her talkin' soon enough. Remember that real bad accident out by the skate rink…"

I tune out as Trevor and Kinsey talk about how bad the accident was. I veer away from them and look at different stuff on the walls: Birds, Angel wings, praying hands, and fancy lettering.

Kinsey calls out to me. "Ay sweetheart, I'm sorry to hear that was your mama."

I nod as a way of thanks. Kinsey walks away to begin scanning and jotting down stuff. Meanwhile Trevor leans against the counter, his eyes slowly go from my feet to my chest. I swallow hard. With his finger he tells me to come to him and, like a little girl, I obey, stopping myself at a good distance in front of him.

"Whatchu think I should get?" he asks.

I place my hand over my chest. Me? He's asking me this? I don't think I should make that decision. I know nothing about him. It's time to be bold again. I'm going to have to talk but before I say anything he says, "I think you'd be cute with a nose ring. A little stud…right…there."

He puts his finger lightly to my left nostril and I tilt my head back at his touch. From behind the counter, Kinsey agrees. Which is expected since it's his shop and he wants my money. I view the price list posted on the wall.

For a nose piercing it ranges from $60 to $80 depending on the ring type and placement. There's a poster showing six different ways the nose can be pierced and nine different types of studs. I've seen people with nose rings before and I always thought they were cool, but I never imagined myself with one. There's enough going on with my face without me having to draw more attention to it. But the idea of getting one sounds…not like me, unpredictable.

"I can tell you're thinking about it," Trevor says. "Get your boy Xave to make you a fake I.D."

I frown and crinkle my eyebrows. What does he mean?

Trevor rubs his chin. "You do know that's what Xavier does right? Why do you think he always has so much cash?"

He's right. Xavier does always seem to have cash, but I thought it was because he worked on computers for people. At least that's what he told me.

"Don't get a fake," Kinsey rubs his full beard. "We can tell…or at least I can. All you need is your parents' consent and for one of them to come with you. You'd be surprised, most parents aren't against it if you ask."

Trevor tells him I'm a PK. Which isn't completely true. Dad's not a full-out preacher yet. Just a youth minister. He only preaches every now and then.

Kinsey doesn't seem surprised. "I get plenty of PK's in here. They try using fakes sometimes or come with an aunt or uncle trying to pass them off as their parent."

Even if I wanted to get one, I don't have that kind of cash and I don't have an aunt or uncle that lives here. Aunt Didi, Mama's sister, lives in Atlanta. Uncle Jerome, my Dad's brother, lives in Las Vegas.

The bell chimes when another customer walks in. The pink-haired girl with a lot of piercings welcomes her in. I don't remember us getting a welcome when we came in, but maybe Trevor's in here all the time.

"Did you decide whatchu gettin', nephew?" Kinsey asks Trevor.

"Well, guess I'll have to go with my original plan since Clove here won't say nothin.'" Trevor smirks at me. "I'm getting her name on my arm."

My eyes feel like they belong to a cartoon character. My jaw drops and the cough drop that's now a tiny sliver falls to the ground. I bend down to pick it up and Kinsey points to a trash can. Him and Trevor share a laugh that sounds more like pigs snorting.

"Relax sweetie," Trevor says. "I'm jokin'."

Who gave him permission to call me sweetie? Trevor tells Kinsey what he's getting. "Number nine on the wall. I trust you cause you've done it before so no need to draw it out. Just need it to say 'Corinthians 4:9'."

Trevor winks at me. Is this why he brought me, so I could watch him get praying hands and a Bible verse tattooed on his arm? Am I supposed to be impressed? Maybe I am a lil bit.

"First Corinthians or Second Corinthians?" Kinsey asks Trevor. "I know which it is but I wanna know if you know."

Trevor has a slight smile on one side of his face. "Which one is it, Clove?"

I honestly don't know so I have to check in my Bible app. Either verse could be something he wants on his arm.

"Depends," I tell him.

"On what?"

"What you're trying to say."

Trevor quotes, "*We are struck down, but not destroyed.*"

Okay, I'm more than a little impressed.

"Second Corinthians," Kinsey and I say at the same time. He either knows because he's tattooed it plenty of times or he's read the Bible.

"What church you go to?" Kinsey asks me.

"God's Light," Trevor answers for me.

Kinsey hits him on the shoulder, a signal that he wanted me to say it for myself. It's evident that Trevor is trying to show me that he knows way more about me than I know about him. He's checking more boxes on my requirement list.

I text Xavier: *Can u make me a fake I. D.?*

## Nine

# *Pierced*

"Are you sure about this?" Xavier whispers to me. Since we live in the same neighborhood, we're meeting at the street light between our houses. It only took Xavier two and a half days to make an I. D. for me and in that time he's drilled me on questions. Now he's having second thoughts as he holds it in his hands, hesitating to give it to me.

"First of all, why are you whispering?" I ask. "It's just us out here. Second, yes, I'm sure."

Xavier pushes his dreads back from his face. He's the exact same complexion as my dad and fits in the category of tall, dark, and handsome. Up until last year, he'd been too nerdy to notice girls noticing him. Kinda like what's been happening to JJ lately. Girls have been paying more attention to both of them and it's so odd.

"JJ is gonna kill me and so is your Pops," he says.

JJ? Why is he worried about JJ? My dad, I can understand, but I plan to get the piercing after school tomorrow when Dad leaves for his ministers' conference. So he won't see it—at least not until he comes back. Gram is staying with me, but I think she'll be more lenient than Dad.

"A nose piercing is very obvious," Xavier says. "You can't hide it like a tattoo. People are going to ask you questions and this whole no talking thing you got goin' on, is not going to work very long."

He has a point, but still I want what I want. Before Xavier agreed to make the ID, I had to tell him why I wanted it. At first, he was going to make me twenty-one years old, but I told him that wasn't necessary. Plus I don't think I could pass for that age. All I want is my nose pierced so I asked Xavier to make me only a year older.

Xavier sighs and hands me the card. "Alright. Look, don't show JJ, and definitely don't show your Pops."

I turn the card over and feel the smoothness of it. Xavier snaps his finger in my face. "Hello? I just asked who's piercing you?"

Oh. Guess I zoned out. "Downtown. Kinsey's shop."

Xavier makes a face. "How do you know Kinsey? You been in his shop?"

"Yeah."

"With who?"

Why so many questions? I don't tell him but he quickly figures it out.

"You went with Trevor to get his new tattoo, didn't you?"

Either Jessa told him or he just knows. I'm gonna guess both.

"When are you going?"

"Tomorrow after school. Jessa's taking me."

"I'm gonna come too. I wanna see if you're actually going to go through with this."

I don't mind if he comes with us. In fact, I sort of want JJ to come too but he'll probably try to talk me out of it.

"You need money?" Xavier asks, already taking out a wad of cash and flipping through it. Whoa! How many fakes does he make in a week? I shake my head, although I appreciate him wanting to take care of me like that. Wait, why is he giving me money when I owe *him*?

I ask him once more how much he wants for the card and begin to take out my own cash. The street light comes on and we stand beside it. Just enough light to see but not enough to be seen.

"Nothing. It's on me. Just let me come with you. I'll take JJ home after school and then I'll ride with you and Jessa."

I don't argue with him on the money nor with letting him tag along. We part ways and return to our houses.

***

"Buttercup," Mama whispers.

"Mama?"

"Sweet Clove. I love you. I miss you."

"Mama?" I hear her, but I can't see her. Where is she? I've only had one dream of Mama after she died and that was the day before I went to school and walked out into that tornado. In that dream there was a tornado that swallowed me up. In the center of the twister was Mama's silhouette.

However, in this dream it's completely the opposite. I can hear Mama's voice, but I can't see her.

"Mama!"

"You are wonderfully made." I hear her voice whisper. There's a sharp pain in my nostril on the left side only. At first it was a quick shoot of pain but now it's throbbing. The room transforms into a wall of hedges. I try turning around but run into a wall of ivy that climbs to the top. I'm in some type of labyrinth. Mama's whispers echo, propelling me to run towards her voice.

"You are wonderfully made." Every time I hear her voice it's *those words*. The very words she'd say to me when I first started struggling with the appearance of my vitiligo.

She whispers again. "God does not look at the outward appearance but what's in the heart."

"Mama, where are you? I want to see you."

Everything starts to fade and my nostril starts to ache even more. Then I hear buzzing. It's the same buzzing that I heard when Trevor got his tattoo. My vision is blurry but Jessa and Xavier's faces come into view.

Jessa clutches her chest. "Oh mah gawd, Clove. Whew. You had us nervous for a minute."

Xavier hands me a soda. "Drink this. You gotta say something when you feel faint like that."

I now recognize where I am. The designs on the wall, the buzzing of someone getting a tattoo. And my nose… oh mercy! My nose hurts so bad. I reach my finger up to touch it but Jessa and Xavier shout "No!" at the same time.

The pink-haired girl I saw the other day is sitting on a short, swivel stool beside me. I focus in on her name tag; *Crystol*

She hands me a mirror and I smile at the small shiny stud in my nose. I like the piercing, it gives me an edge. Crystol tells me how to care for it and then gives me a fact sheet that lists all the do's and don'ts. She also gives me some cleaning solution.

Jessa and Xavier lean in to take a closer look. "Ya know," Jessa says to Xavier. "It actually looks good on her."

Xavier folds his arms over his chest. "I don't like it."

Jessa smacks him in the stomach with the back of her hand. It makes a *thwack* sound.

"Tell me you didn't do this because Trevor said you'd be cute with one." Jessa says.

I glare at Jessa. She couldn't keep a cat in the bag if she tried.

Xavier's eyes are like an owl's. "Seriously? That's why you did this? Cause of him? Wow, Clove."

I put the mirror down. "No, Xave. I did it for me. You only live once, right? So I'm living."

Jessa and Xavier are both silent for a moment but then Jessa grins. "I really like it. Maybe I should get one too."

Xavier rolls his eyes. "Oh, god. Here we go."

Jessa clicks her tongue in annoyance. "Geez Dad, can you relax?"

"I *am* relaxed."

"You're not. You're being a fun snatcher."

"I'm the most fun person ever," Xavier argues.

"You are not," Jessa argues back.

Crystol ignores their old-couple bickering and says to me, "Clean the area twice a day. Oh, and no makeup near the nose. I told you that, right?"

I nod.

"You know you're going to have to be extra careful, even to blow your nose now," Xavier informs me.

"Shuddup, Xave," Jessa snaps.

He ignores Jessa and continues. "And you'll get more bats in the cave trying to be careful."

"Shut. Up." Jessa says through gritted teeth then tells me to drink more soda. Next she pulls out some crackers from her purse and tells me to eat a few. She asks Crystol if she can get her nose pierced too.

Xavier goes outside, declaring he can't stand to watch.

"Wimp," Jessa calls after him and then giggles. While Crystol goes to the cash register, Jessa asks a question I know she's been longing to ask. "So what's up with you and Trevor?"

I glance over her shoulder at Trevor's Uncle Kinsey who's busy tattooing someone. I doubt he can hear us over the buzzing.

"Have you two talked on the phone or are you still giving one-liners and one-word answers?" Jessa asks.

"We've kinda been texting."

Jessa seems like she's debating with herself. I know she wants to tell me something but before I can ask her what happened between her and Trevor, Xavier comes back inside and hands me a phone. "Here. JJ wants to talk to you."

Jessa's facial expression completely changes. "Xave! What are we? Five again? Why would you call him? See, you're a fun snatcher."

I take Xavier's phone. Then he and Jessa go outside to argue some more. Xavier is calm but Jessa's hands and arms move like she's on fire. They fight like a couple even though they're not. Both say they're not interested in each other but I'm not sure I believe it.

I put the phone to my ear. JJ's baby sister is babbling and banging on something in the background.

"Adah," JJ calls to her. "Ssshhhh. I'm on the phone."

"Hey," I say.

"Hey," he says. The background banging resumes. "Sorry, hold on." I wait for him to tell me how he can't believe I got my nose pierced.

"Can you come over after you're done? I want to see your nose ring."

I bring the phone to my face to make sure Xavier called the right JJ. I can't believe that's all he has to say.

"Okay, I'll have Jessa bring me over."

"See you soon," he says before hanging up. Suddenly, I don't want to wait for Jessa to get her nose pierced. I want to see JJ.

Outside, I give Xavier back his phone. "Can we come back for your piercing another day, Jess? I'm ready to go and JJ wants me to come over so he can see my nose ring."

Jessa and Xavier exchange glances and a small smile tugs on the side of Xavier's mouth. I don't know what those looks mean, but I brush past them and head to Jessa's car.

Once we're all back in the car, Jessa asks, "Are there any more spots available on the college tour? 'Cause I think I want to go."

"Last I heard there were two spots left on the tour. Both of you should come. It'll be fun."

"I'm down," Xavier says, "Send me the form and I'll get it back to you."

"Same," Jessa says. "I'm in."

A sense of relief goes through me at the idea that I'll get to spend spring break with all of my besties.

## Ten

# Fromage Grillé

Jessa drops me off at JJ's house. Before I can knock, he opens the door wearing a sleeveless gray shirt that draws my eyes directly to his well-sculpted arms. On his shoulder, his sister sleeps with her little lips slightly parted. So cute!

He steps back, giving me space to walk inside. His youngest brother, Caleb, runs to me.

"Clove, are you still sad? Mommy's been sad too. Wanna play with me?"

"Shhhh," JJ whispers to Caleb and shuts the door behind me.

Caleb murmurs an apology and then holds up a memory game. "Will you play with me?"

I nod. "Yes, but first I need to use the ladies room."

As I wash my hands, I admire the shimmering stud in my nostril. It's very, very tiny and not too noticeable. Hopefully Dad won't make a big deal out of it.

When I leave the bathroom, Caleb is waiting for me with the memory cards all laid out on the carpet.

"Jonah went to put Adah in her bed," he says. "I already turned two cards over so it's your turn."

I turn two cards over with no match.

"Hey." Caleb peers at me. "There's something on your nose. I think it's a boogie. I'll go get a tissue for you."

He leaves the room and I chuckle a bit. So much for it not being obvious. Caleb hands me the tissue but I don't wipe. He takes a closer look at my nose. "Hmmm, that's weird, it's sparkly. Maybe it's just a piece of glitter or something."

I bring his active mind back to our game. We play for about five minutes before Caleb tells me he's hungry.

The house is quiet. "Where is everybody?" I ask.

"Mommy went to the grocery store to buy groceries for dinner and JJ prolly fell asleep. Zach is at basketball practice and Papa is still at work in Memphis. Can you fix me something to eat?"

Me? Fix food? "Um…sure. I guess I can try." Baking is one thing, but cooking is another thing altogether.

"Can you make a cake?"

"No cake before dinner," I tell him. I'm not yet ready to start baking again anyway. I check the refrigerator to search for something simple he would eat. Cheese, butter, and bread. *Grilled cheese.* I heat the cast iron skillet as Caleb sits at the counter and watches.

"Are you making *fromage grillé?*" he tries to say in French. I vaguely remember JJ saying something like that for grilled cheese.

"If that means grilled cheese, then yes." I wait for the butter to melt, then plop the sandwich into the skillet. While I'm searching for a spatula, I get a message.

**Trevor**: *Let me see it.*

News travels fast. Guess his uncle already told him I was in the shop today. I take a selfie making sure to get my nose ring shimmering in the light. I don't like the first photo so I try again and move towards the sunlight. The next photo is better, but then I decide to take my hair down from the French braids and pull it over to one side of my face. Much better.

"Um…Clove," Caleb says. "Don't you have to flip it or somethin'?"

Oh yeah, the grilled cheese. I run back over to the skillet and flip the sandwich. It's slightly burnt, but that's okay because there's still the other side.

I go back to picture taking and try making different faces with my lips: fish lips, pouty, snarled lip and then one with my lips slightly parted. I pick one and send it to Trevor.

"Is something burning?" Caleb asks.

I sniff. Holy smokes! I grab an oven mitt and remove the pan from the stove, tossing the now blackened grilled cheese on the counter. Caleb runs to open the door. Thankfully the smoke alarm doesn't go off because it would definitely wake Adah.

I rinse the pan in the sink and yelp as steam rises into the air, the water causing the pan to make a sizzling noise. I fan the air. "Sorry, Caleb. I'll try again and pay attention next time." I search for another, smaller pan and start the process over.

**Trevor**: *U look hot!*

**Me**: *Thanks*

**Trevor**: *Ur dad see?*

**Me**: *Not yet. Not at home.*

**Trevor**: *Where u at? Let me come scoop u.*

The word "scoop" gets on my nerves. I am not a dessert. But I'll let it slide this time.

**Me**: *Where are we going?*

**Trevor**: *U tell me.*

Why'd he ask if he doesn't know where we're going? He's not coming to my house and I'm not inviting him over to JJ's.

The smoke alarm beeps and Caleb gets down from the counter stool to open the door again.

Once more I remove the skillet from the stove. The house smells of burnt bread and cheese. I can't believe I've done this twice.

"What on Earth?" Mrs. Jourdan says, walking into the house. Zach follows her with bags of groceries. Both of them begin to open all the windows. Meanwhile JJ brings a distraught Adah downstairs. Her face is wet with tears. I feel terrible that I've made such a mess of things and woke poor Adah from her sleep.

"What happened?" Mrs. Jourdan says, taking the baby.

To my horror, Caleb explains everything. "Clove was trying to make me *fromage grillé* but she burnt it up twice because she was sending pictures on her phone."

You can always trust a four-year-old to tell the truth when you really don't want them to.

Mrs. Jourdan starts laughing. She holds up the grilled cheese sandwiches as if they're giant playing cards and throws it to Zach. He catches it and then throws it to JJ.

"My turn," Caleb declares.  All of them are playing frisbee with my blackened grilled cheese sandwiches.

"Grilled cheese makes a great toy," Caleb exclaims.

I try not to laugh but it *is* kind of funny. My dad sends me a message asking when I'm coming home. How does he know I'm not home? I thought he was out of town already.

"Clove, would you like to stay for dinner? James is cooking," Mrs. Jourdan tells me, happy that her husband is cooking tonight. From what I know, Mr. Jourdan once worked in a restaurant in France and is a pretty good cook.

My dad sends me another text letting me know his flight got delayed. Oh shoot! He's going to see my nose piercing tonight! I am not ready for his lecture.

**Dad**: *Gram cooked. Come home so we can eat together before I leave.*

I twist my lips and tap my foot, trying to think. "Um, my dad just texted. He says Gram cooked for us."

"Oh yeah? What'd Gram cook?" Mrs. Jourdan asks.

I announce the food as Dad texts it to me. He sends multiple messages instead of just one, so I have to read slowly as each one appears. "Fried fish… green beans…hush puppies… yams….and….and I guess that's it." The messages stop but then another one appears.

"Mac n cheese," I say finally.

Zach raises his hand as though we're in school. "I vote we go to Clove's house 'cause I'm hungry now and I'm not tryna wait on dad to get here."

Mrs. Jourdan reads her phone and then sighs as she puts it down on the counter. "Your dad is running late. We'll need to cook for ourselves."

"Just come over," I tell them. "Gram hardly ever makes small meals. I'm sure there's plenty." I'm thinking that if they come over, it might delay Dad's wrath.

Mrs. Jourdan puts her hand gently on my wrist. "Honey, these are three hungry boys and I don't know if Gram has enough food. It's okay. We'll be fine." She leans in close to my face just as Jessa, Xavier, and Caleb had done.

"Hmmmm," she says. "Maybe you should stay over here and I'll order takeout. I have a feeling if you go home, you might be in for a while."

Zach scrunches his nose. "Hold up! Clove's gram cooked all that food and we don't get to eat because Clove got her nose pierced? How is that fair? I'm seriously hungry. She's gotta go home eventually."

He has a point. I can't hide here forever. "Thanks for trying to buy me some time, Mrs. Jourdan, but I'm gonna own this. I made the choice and I think I know what the consequences will be. There's no sense in you ordering food when I know there's plenty at home."

Everyone gapes at me for several seconds. Then Zach interrupts the silence. "Okay, so are we going to your house or what?" He's still only thinking about food.

Mrs. Jourdan answers for me. "Clove, how about I have Jonah take you home? If there's enough food, you can pack us up some plates and Jonah can bring them back. You're going to need to talk to your dad."

"Yes ma'am."

JJ takes the keys from his mom. He opens the Explorer passenger door for me. We're silent as we drive. He hasn't said anything about my nose stud and I've been wondering what he thinks.

"Soooo, whaddaya think?" I ask him.

"What do I think about what?"

"Was me gettin' a nose ring predictable?"

It takes him a few seconds to respond. "Is that why you got it? Because I said you were predictable?"

"No." That's a half lie. JJ saying that was part of the reason; the other part was Trevor saying I'd look good in one.

"Clove, I didn't mean that you were predictable in a bad way. I just meant that I know you. That's all."

Oh. Well still, he said it and regardless of how he meant it, I'm tired of being boring and predictable. I peer down at my nails and pick at my dry cuticles. I've never worn anything on them other than clear polish or sometimes a pale pink. I am predictable. I haven't even changed my hairstyle from the two French braids that Gram put them in last week. I'd re-braided them, but still, it's the same style.

"Clove, you're not boring. If anything, you're multifaceted. You only need to explore who you are more."

"What do you mean? What do you know about my facets?"

A smile forms on his mouth and for the first time I realize how cute it is.

"For starters, you can bake. You can't cook, but you can bake. I think you should explore that more. I also think you're a good writer. That paper you wrote on Maya Angelou was actually quite good."

I feel myself blushing. "Thanks," I say and begin chewing my lower lip.

"You ever thought about writing poetry?" he asks.

I shake my head. "Not really."

"You should try it. I think you might be good at it."

Maybe he's on to something. I haven't really tried writing as a hobby. Mama used to write, but I think it was mostly prayers in her journals from time to time.

"All I'm saying," JJ continues. "Is that I know you're far from boring."

Hearing him say that means a whole lot, but I still want to know what he thinks about my piercing. "Do you think I shouldn't have gotten my nose pierced? Do you not like it?"

I realize I sound superficial and insecure, but maybe I am a little bit.

"Why does it matter what I think?" He asks so coolly that I'm not so sure he wants me to answer. It shouldn't matter, but it does. I want his approval and I haven't the foggiest idea why because I don't care what Jessa and Xavier think nearly as much.

"Your opinion matters to me," I finally answer.

JJ taps his thumb on the top of the steering wheel. "Do you like it?" he asks.

Why can't he just give me his opinion like other people? *Because he's not like other people,* I answer myself.

"Yes. I don't regret it, but maybe I sorta feel bad for the way I went about getting it."

JJ nods his head slowly. "I think that's all that matters, your opinion and how you feel about it, but if you really need my opinion, I'll give it to you."

He keeps driving and I wait for him to give me his opinion. When we get to my house, he still hasn't said anything. The suspense is killing me.

"Oh my gosh, J. Are you gonna tell me or not?"

He sucks his jaws in as if holding back a laugh. "Nope. You don't need my opinion. You *want* it."

Ugh! He frustrates me. I shove his shoulder. "Chump!"

# Eleven

# He Loves Me Not

Xavier was right. I'm getting all kinds of gawks, comments, and questions about my nose today at school. I didn't think it would be this big of a deal.

At lunch Tisha walks over to our table.

"I really like your nose ring, Clove," she says, pulling up a chair next to JJ. He looks at the chair, at her and then back to the chair again. Like me, he has to be thinking, *why on Earth is she sitting with us?* To make matters worse, she brings raggedy Mars with her. Now there are five people at our table and even though there's plenty of room, it's feeling a little cramped.

"Thanks," I reply, dryly.

Trevor pulls up a seat next to me. I eye his seat like JJ did Tisha's.

"What are you and Trevor going as for the dance?" Tisha asks me.

"Um, what?" I have no idea what she's talking about. First of all, I hadn't officially asked Trevor to the dance. Second of all, what does she mean by *going as?*

"You know it's superhero-themed, right? Jonah and I are going as Batgirl and Robin," she grins. When did JJ decide that he was going with her? He said she was missing some chocolate chips. Personally, I think she's missing all of them. She ain't nothing but a wafer.

I send a message to him with my eyes, cocking my head to the side. Code:

*What's going on?*

He stares down at his food like it might be talking to him.

Trevor turns towards me and traces his finger down my arm. "So what are we going as, sweetie?"

I hadn't asked him to go anywhere with me or given him permission to give me a pet name. Which reminds me, Tisha didn't call me Pinky. She actually said my name this time.

My mind races to think of superheroes so I can answer Trevor but I got nothin'.

"You could be Storm," Tisha suggests. "You got that black and white thing going for you already. You just need white hair."

All of us all gape at her, including Mars who rolls her eyes then shakes her head. Tisha couldn't raise her IQ if she stood on a chair!

Trevor keeps running his finger up and down my arm. "Don't really matter how we dress, as long as it's easy to get into, and easy to get out of."

He watches carefully for my reaction. I'm uncertain of what emotion to show. It should be anger, but no guy has ever been so bold with me before. It's an interesting change.

This time, it's JJ's eyes that send a message, only it's not for me, it's like a death glare to Trevor. Mars gets everyone's attention by asking Xavier to the dance.

He turns her down, like I knew he would. Not many Seniors want to attend the Sadie Hawkins dance when they have prom.

Mars clicks her tongue and moves to another table. I wish Tisha and Trevor would do the same. Having them here feels like an alien invasion.

Trevor is cute though, so I guess I need to put a little more thought into this dance. Do I wanna go or not? And do I wanna go with Trevor? Since I'm currently grounded forever, I may have to sneak out of the house.

After JJ dropped me off last night, I packed up plates of food quickly, covering them with foil and finding plastic containers for everything. As I expected, there was plenty of food. JJ came inside with me, for which I was grateful. Dad didn't miss a thing. He noticed my nose right away but waited until JJ left to say anything about it.

I think having JJ there gave him extra time to think about what he was going to say. I hadn't done anything like this before so he chose one word to start his lecture.

"Why?" he asked.

"Dad, it's *my* face. Why can't I do what I want?"

"How'd you get it? Who took you?"

I didn't want to rat out my friends. So I blurted the first thing that came to my mind. "I got a fake I.D. and went by myself."

"You're lying and I know you're lying. Sister Brenda said she saw you, Jessa and Xavier coming out of the tattoo shop. It's really not even about the nose ring. It's how you went about getting it. Do you plan to go drinking with your fake I.D.?"

"No, I don't wanna drink." I said. "Why would you even ask me that? After what happened to Mama, you think I'm gonna buy alcohol?"

His assumption infuriated me so much that I didn't even eat dinner with them last night. Instead, I went straight to my room. I felt like crying but there were no tears. With my face buried in the pillow, I screamed.

"So…" Trevor licks his fork. "Have you seen the person that hit your mom?"

No one has dared to ask me that question. The person that hit her survived with only a broken leg. That's it. She still has her life and I hate her for it.

It feels like the whole cafeteria has gone silent like they're all waiting for the answer, including JJ and Xavier. Either they think he's nuts for asking or they want to know the answer too.

Trevor glances at my face. "You don't hafta answer. I'm just wonderin' cause I heard she survived. The news said she had two kids or somethin' like that."

Two kids? How could a mom do that to another mom? Isn't that violating some kind of mom code?

I clench my jaw. "No. Why would I do that?" I feel anger coursing through my body but I'm trying to be calm.

Trevor shrugs, "Thought y'all church people was all about forgiveness. Ain't that what the good book say?"

I'm done talking. I start packing up my things but then Tisha reaches her hand out to me.

"Wait. Um, do you want to go skating tonight?" she asks.

I stop packing. First of all, she touched my hand. The only time she ever touched me was to push me in the mud. Second, she's inviting me to go somewhere with her. Third, it's skating. This means going back to the place where the accident happened.

Tisha adds, "Just thought it'd be nice if we could hang out. Get to know each other."

Get to know each other? We've known each other since elementary school. And she never needed to know me in order to push me down or call me names. Me and her don't do hangouts.

"I'm grounded. But thanks." I get up and throw away my trash, ignoring someone who calls out that I get a six on the bubble butt scale.

Too many questions go through my mind so I decide to go outside and sit at one of the empty picnic tables that's covered in bird poo. All this crap about the dance, the drunk woman with the kids, and then Tisha's dumb invitation. Why'd she asked me to go with her in the first place?

I really want to skate again, but going back to the skate rink, thinking about how I'm the reason mama is gone, I just can't go back. Not now, maybe not ever. I will never forgive the drunk driver. Never.

I inhale deeply. Something smells good. To the left of me is a honeysuckle bush. Mama once showed me how a sweet, tiny drop of nectar would appear if you carefully pinched and pulled at the end of the bud.

Carefully, I take a flower off of the bush. I don't see the bees, but I can hear them buzzing.

I do exactly as Mama taught me and try to get that single drop of nectar. Unfortunately, I'm too forceful and end up ripping the bloom. I throw it down and take another off the bush.

Five blooms later, the bell rings but I stay put, determined to get the nectar. Behind me the door to the cafeteria squeaks open.

"Are you playing a game of he loves you, he loves you not?" JJ asks.

I sort of laugh, but it's one of those laughs that escapes you when something is semi-funny. I pick up my things and walk back into the cafeteria. "You think I'm wondering if Trevor loves me?"

"No. Thought you were wondering if God loves you."

"Ha! That's funny, JJ." I put my backpack straps over my shoulder before throwing the last bloom on the ground. "God doesn't love me."

# Twelve

## Honeysuckles

I'm not only grounded but I have to do whatever my dad says. Today I'm washing his car, and tomorrow after church, I have to reorganize his office bookshelf.

It's a warm, sunny Saturday. We're in full spring mode even though the vernal equinox is a few days away. Though it's nice outside, I feel like there's a cloud over me. Any sliver of hope or warmth I get is cloaked in a heaviness that I can't seem to shake.

I fill a bucket with soapy water and grab an extra-large sponge. Soap suds hit me on the cheek when I plop the sponge in the bucket. I used way too much soap.

"Good Morning, Clove."

Startled, I turn around and accidentally fling JJ with soap suds and water. It gets all over his shirt and shorts.

"Oh my gosh JJ, I'm so sorry!"

JJ scans his wet clothes.

"That'll cool him off," Xavier says walking up my driveway. "Usain Bolt over here decided to run five miles instead of three today."

Dang. Five miles? I can't even run one.

"Why aren't you breaking a sweat like JJ?" I ask Xavier.

"I overslept and haven't started yet," he says to me. To JJ, he says, "You can start lifting without me. I'll be back in thirty." Xavier begins jogging down the street, leaving me and JJ standing in the driveway.

Walking towards the garage, I look for a towel so JJ can dry himself off. But when I return to the driveway, he's gone.

"JJ?" I look around.

Did he go home? I check down the street but don't see him anywhere. Suddenly cold water splashes me in the back, causing my whole body to tense. "Ahhhh, ahhh, c-c-cold…cold!"

JJ snickers.

"Jonah Jourdan, I swear!" I yell.

With the hose still in his hand, he takes a few steps backwards. "Don't take another step," he taunts. I step on the hose stopping the water supply. We make eye contact. And then we both know: It's. About. To go. Down.

He drops the hose and I chase him around the car, not knowing what I'm going to do if I catch him. For right now, the chase is fun. We pause for a moment; at an impasse. I can see him straight through the back window. I move an inch right and he moves the other way. He moves an inch and I move the opposite way. One of us has to surrender, but it ain't gonna be me.

I crouch down low, quietly crawling around the car. When I see his legs, I reach out to grab one, but all I get is air because he escapes quickly.

"You're not good at sneaking up on people," he says with a laugh.

"Get back here you….you…scurvy knave!"

"Scurvy knave?" JJ laughs. "Really? Have you been reading Shakespeare?"

Realizing I just quoted *Romeo and Juliet*, I laugh too. That makes me think of the time we went sledding and Xavier had to pee but there were no bathrooms. So JJ said, "To pee or not to pee." It was so stupid, but we were so cold and so tired that we all laughed hysterically out of sheer exhaustion.

"I know what you're thinking about," he says. "That time Xavier had to go in the snow and later Zach thought someone had brought snow cones."

Thinking about that whole trip makes me double over in laughter.

"I haven't seen you laugh like that in a while," JJ says.

He's right. I don't think I've laughed this hard in a long time and it feels good. I seem to open up more when he's around. First talking and now laughing.

Beads of water cover his glasses. He takes them off and tries to find a dry spot on his shirt to clean them. I look at myself to check for the same and find a dry sleeve. "Here," I give him my left shoulder. "Use my sleeve. It's dry."

He takes my sleeve and begins drying his glasses. For a long time JJ and I used to be the same height, but now it seems he's several inches taller.

His light-colored eyelashes and the freckles that cover his nose and cheeks are picturesque. The water has made his hair curl up even more. I've always wanted to touch his hair, but I've been too afraid to ask. I wonder if he's ever wanted to touch mine. Hair. My hair! I reach up and check to see if it got wet.

"I did not get your hair wet," he says, putting his glasses back on. "I made sure of that."

I smile. "Your mama taught you well."

He taps the side of his head. "It's ingrained in my brain; never get a black woman's hair wet."

We're all up in each other's personal space. So much so that I can smell his perspiration.

JJ takes a step back. "Sorry, I probably smell sweaty."

It doesn't bother me, but I scrunch up my nose just to mess with him. "Go shower!"

He lifts his arm to fan the air towards me. "Smell it. That's all hard work right there."

"Ew!" I push him away.

We laugh for a moment. "Hey," he says. "You still waking up at five?"

"Yeah. Why?"

"Will you come somewhere with me tomorrow?"

"Where and what time?" I don't even think about the fact that I might not be able to go because I'm grounded. But it's JJ; he wouldn't ask if it weren't somewhere I could go.

"There's a midway point between our houses. You know what I'm talking about, right? At Hollow and Chickaree?"

"Yeah."

"Can you meet me there by 5:45?" he asks.

"Are you gonna be running? Cause I'm not running. And you'll get there before me."

"It's okay," he says. "I'll wait for you."

Something about the way he said that makes my cheeks feel warm. JJ peeks over my shoulder and I turn around to see what he's looking at.

"Hold on a sec," he says.

He disappears between our house and the next door neighbor's. What is he doing? If he had to pee, he could've come inside.

I go back to washing Dad's car. He'll want it clean before he gets back Sunday evening. Truthfully, I could've waited until Sunday to wash his car. It's not like he'll know if I washed it today or not. Or maybe Gram would tell him if—

"Clove."

I jump at the sound of JJ's voice once again. My heart is racing but calms down a little when I see what's in his hand. Honeysuckles; a bushel of them.

"Your neighbor has some in their yard. Don't tell them I stole these." As he extends his hand to me, I notice it's red.

"Did you get stung by a bee?" I ask him.

"Yes. Now please take these so I can go cry like a man."

Biting my lip to suppress a laugh, I take the flowers. Good thing he's not allergic to bees. Grabbing his hand, I lead him inside the house so I can help him remove the stinger.

Gram smiles from ear to ear when she sees JJ. She's always liked my friends and enjoys having them over. "Hey there, young man. Have some pancakes." It wasn't a question, it was a command. When Gram is cooking, she never asks if you *want* to eat.

"Uh, yes ma'am, I'll be happy to have some as soon as Clove is done pretending to be a doctor. Clove, it didn't leave a stinger behind. I already checked."

"Well why'd you let me drag you inside then?"

"Because once a bee stings you, it sends out a message to its fellow bees to come and help. So the bee that stung me was going to call for reinforcement and—"

I put my finger to his lips. "Shhhh." He's always so full of information.

"Why'd you even risk getting stung?" I ask him.

"I want you to try again," he says.

"Try what again?"

"To see if God loves you."

# Thirteen

## *Poetic*

Dr. O'dea's office is warm and suffocating. I'm sitting on a cozy, light blue couch, listening to water trickling from a fountain. The fountain is supposed to be for relaxation, but I find it annoying. A faux iris plant resting in a silver pot sits on a sofa table that's underneath a painting of —I don't know what that's a painting of—perhaps just a painting of paint. Dr. O'dea sits on an oversized cream-colored chair, jotting notes on her notepad. Her glasses have fallen to the tip of her nose, where she lets them rest. She smiles a friendly smile and begins talking to me in her thick Jamaican accent. "How you been, Miss Clove?"

I don't feel like talking, so I reply with a shrug.

"Yer fahder tinks you are depressed. Are you depressed?"

How should I know? Isn't she supposed to tell me that? I shrug again. Watching paint dry on a wall would be better than these sessions. I suppose it gives me some reprieve from the mundane school-to-work schedule. Instead of meeting with her only on Wednesdays, my Dad added Mondays to our sessions.

"I like dat nose ring."

"Thanks." I cover my mouth. I hadn't meant to say that. I'd planned on not talking at all but I guess manners are entrenched in me. It's like an automatic response when someone pays me a compliment.

"Did you take any pictures of yer'self? Any...what do you young people call dem? Selfies?"

I nod.

"May I see dem?"

I nod. When I come into Dr. O'dea's office, first thing I have to do is surrender my phone. So Dr. O'dea takes it out of the little lockbox and sits beside me.

"Show me," she says, handing me my phone. I unlock it and navigate to my photos. The first photo that appears is one JJ sent me after our run yesterday.

I met him exactly where he told me to meet him, at the corner of Chickory and Hollow. Since Daylight Savings Time had arrived, the sky was still dark and completely filled with stars. JJ was waiting for me just like he said he would.

"How long you been waiting?" I asked when I arrived.

"Not long. Did you walk or run?"

I gave him a knowing look. He knew I wasn't about that running life.

He half laughed as he scanned my attire. The morning air was nippy but JJ had on basketball shorts with a tight long sleeve shirt. I, on the other hand, was bundled in every warm thing I could find.

"Cold?" he asked.

"Aren't you?" His shorts and long sleeves had me confused about what weather he was dressed for.

Instead of answering my question, he tapped his watch. "Okay, so don't be mad at me, but we need to run now."

"What?"

He took off running. At first I just watched his stride but when he turned the corner, I realized I needed to catch up.

Once I caught up with him, we matched each other stride for stride. For a couple minutes I was fine, but then I started to breathe harder and felt like I needed a break.

"Breathe like this," JJ ran backwards to show me how he breathed. I mimicked it and it helped a little but I still wanted to stop.

"Almost there," he said.

I didn't know where "there" was, but I kept running with him. We were running east underneath a path of street lights, but then he deviated from the path and slowed down to go up a steep, grassy hill.

I contemplated it because it seemed like a giant. My energy and stamina had left me. There was no way my body was going to allow me up that hill. It was too big and if we were going all the way to the top, I was sure I'd collapse before making it there.

JJ extended his hand to me. "Come on, Clove. I got you. Trust me."

I trusted him, so I reached my arm out and his hand firmly grasped mine. He pulled me up to the top, doing all the work, because my feet and body were done.

My heart felt like it was beating out of my chest, my throat was raw from trying to take in so much of the cold air, and my lips were on the verge of bleeding from being so dry. But when we finally reached the top of the hill—which seemed like a mini Mount Everest in my eyes, the stars were gradually fading and the sky above the treetops was like a lighter shade of blue. It was beautiful, well worth the run and the climb.

JJ leaned against a tree desolate of its leaves. Spring had come early, but that tree either didn't get the memo or had gone on to greener pastures.

I began to understand why JJ wore shorts. Sweat fell from my forehead and down my temple. I removed my hoodie and hung it over one of the branches of the dead tree. Then I sat down and leaned my back against the tree bark.

JJ sat next to me. "You should probably keep your sweatshirt on. Your body is perspiring so it can cool you off. But that also means your pores are open. You're going to be very cold in a moment."

I didn't listen at first and let my sweatshirt stay on the branch while JJ continued talking. "There are three types of twilight," he said. "Astronomical, Nautical, and Civil. Right now we're in the Nautical. The sun is between twelve and eighteen degrees below the horizon."

I didn't quite understand what he meant but I was sure that he was right. The sky and the stars were his thing. He knew all about them. We sat silently for a few minutes, enjoying the sounds of the morning. Birds chirped, insects made sounds, and somewhere a rooster crowed. It wasn't quiet around us, yet it was peaceful.

After several minutes, I began to shiver and took my sweatshirt down from the tree.

Knowing he was right, JJ smiled to himself.

"Do you always come here when you run?" I asked. If he did, I could see why he ran every morning.

His eyes remained focused on the skyline above the trees. "Not all the time."

I listened to the sounds of the birds chirping. They were singing like crazy as if they were cheering the daylight on.

"Those birds are really happy." I said.

"If you'd spent the whole night in the cold darkness, wouldn't you be happy to see the light?" He looked at me and I got lost in his eyes again. Not wanting to stare too long, I focused on the sky. The shades of blue were becoming pink at the horizon, something like a different version of a rainbow.

For I don't know how long, we watched the sky change as the sun began to ascend. My mouth parted at the beauty before me. It was amazing. JJ had a smile forming at the corners of his mouth. "What do you think?" he asked.

I sat there in awe, breathless but not from the run. "I love it," I whispered. "It's like watching the Earth get kissed by the sun: an awakening."

My eyes were focused on the view but I could feel JJ's eyes on me.

"That sounds poetic, Clove. I think you should write that down."

We stayed until the sun was above the horizon. After I got back home, I decided to take his advice and wrote a poem in the journal Dr. O'dea gave me. It was the first thing I'd written that wasn't a feeling of anger.


Dr. O'dea points to the silhouetted photo that JJ took of me watching the sunrise. "Tell me 'bout dis pic'cha," she says.

I think it's self-explanatory really but I briefly tell her how JJ and I went running and walking to watch the sunrise.

"Who is JJ?" she asks.

"He's my best friend."

She nods, then she swipes—without permission—to the picture where me and JJ took a selfie together or maybe it's called a twosie or something. I don't know. Anyway, in the photo, we're close together and smiling for the camera.

"Look at all that pretty red hair he has. He's very handsome. You say the two of you are just friends?"

"Yes, just friends."

Dr. O'dea has amusement in her eyes. "Hmmmm," she says, giving me my phone back. "Did you write any ting down in yer jernal?"

"Poetry." Or I should say I attempted poetry. JJ made me think I was a poet when we got back to my house but on paper it didn't look so great.

"Would you like to tell me about it?" Dr. O'dea asks.

I reach inside my backpack, removing the journal she gave me.

I turn directly to the poem I wrote yesterday and begin to recite.

*"Your light shines down on me*
*like kisses to awaken my soul,*
*warming me with your touch,*
*healing me with your love.*
*Your brightness is a lamp,*
*making me glow and gleam with every move you make.*
*Your beauty is obsessive, enthralling and captivating.*
*I'm in awe of you."*

I can feel Dr. O'dea beaming at me. "Well, Miss Clove, it sounds like you are in love, chile."

I shake my head. "I'm not in love. I don't think I understand love. Right now, I can only love the sunrise I saw. That's all I was referring to in the poem."

Dr. O'dea nods slowly again. She doesn't believe me.

## Fourteen



Dad tries to make small talk with me by asking me about my session with Dr. O'dea. I don't want to talk to him. Besides, whatever I discuss with Dr. O'dea is supposed to stay private.

"Phone," he says, holding out his hand. Since I'm grounded he's keeping my phone. I don't know why he gave it back to me in the first place. It's not like I can use it in Dr. O'dea's office. Maybe he wanted me to have it in case I needed him. Who knows. Parents are weird.

As soon as I hand it to him, my screensaver lights up allowing Dad to see the photo JJ took of me watching the sunrise.

"When'd you take this?" he asks looking at the photo.

Now I have to say something. "I didn't take it, JJ did. We went running yesterday morning. Am I allowed to do that? Or would you prefer to keep me like a veal, caged and in the dark?"

"Don't get smart with me. I was only asking because it's a nice photo."

Instantly, I feel bad for the way I responded. "Thanks," I mumble. When I get home, I return to my desk to finish my homework.

Dad knocks on my door but I don't respond so he comes in seconds later. He sits down at the end of my bed. "I need you to do something for me."

I keep writing.

Dad taps my shoulder. "Clove, be respectful. Stop what you're doing and look at me."

I put my pencil down.

"Sister Brenda, is having an Easter Supper for her family. Your mom always made a few desserts for her and she wanted to know if you would make them. You're the only one I know that can make things like your mother used to. You know her recipes."

I do know her recipes, but I've never made them by myself. Why should I do anything for Sister Brenda? She's the one who snitched on me about my nose ring.

"Can't they make it at the bakery? Or can I give Miss Brenda the recipes so she can make it herself?"

Dad exhales slowly. "She's requested you specifically."

This has to be some kind of plan to get me out of whatever depression or funk he thinks I'm in.

"She's willing to pay you."

That gets my attention. "How much?"

"How much do you want? It'll be two pies and two cakes. One Chess, one Chocolate Chess, Pineapple Upside Down, and a Strawberry Poke Cake."

Making a Strawberry Poke cake would be new, but I've made Pineapple cake plenty of times. People used to rave about Mama's Strawberry Poke cake. Whenever she made it, the whole house would smell so good that I could hardly wait for it to cool. Whenever the bakery tried copying her recipe it didn't come out right. Plus it wasn't always a very pretty cake. It needed to be put into a casserole dish because it was so messy. Messy but really good.

If I can do this right, I can make some money before going on the trip, assuming Ms. Brenda will pay me in advance. "I'll get back to you on the price," I tell Dad. I need to calculate how much it would cost for all the ingredients plus enough for me to make a profit.

"They won't need it until Easter. You have plenty of time to do some practice runs if you need to. I volunteer to be a taste tester."

Of course he volunteers himself.

"Sister Brenda said she'll pay you upon completion. So you'll need to buy your supplies with your savings."

Doggone it!

"Dad, can I see my phone? I need to text Jessa about something for school."

He takes my phone out of his pocket. "No texting. Call her."

"Yes, sir."

I dial Jessa but it rings once and goes to voicemail. "Hey Jess, call me back." I hang up. To my dad, I say, "She didn't answer, so can I keep my phone for a few minutes to see if she calls back?"

Dad folds his arms over his chest, thinking. He could easily take the phone with him and let me know if she calls. But for whatever reason, he gives me grace. "Ten minutes," he says. "I want your phone back in ten. You got it?"

As soon as dad leaves, Jessa texts me: *Sorry couldn't answer when u called. I'm somewhere really loud. What's up?*

**Me**: *Need an outfit for the dance.*

**Jessa**: Are *u still going with Trevor??*

I'm not 100 percent on going with Trevor. But at this point he's my first choice since JJ is going with Tisha. Not that I wanted to go with JJ, just…well anyway, it's more about the thrill of going to my first real dance that's not at church.

**Me**: *Yes. Need ideas.*

There's no reply from Jessa at first. But then a message comes through.

**Jessa**: *It should be something easy.*

**Me**: *That's what Trevor said.*

**Jessa**: *He said that???*

**Me**: *He said easy to get into and easy to get out of.*

Jessa sends a surprised-face emoji.

**Jessa**: *Wow. I meant easy as in putting it together. Idk, girl. U sure u want to go with him? Can u ask someone else? Is ur dad letting u go?*

**Me**: *Who else could I go with? No, I haven't asked my dad if I can go.*

Now she sends a worried face emoji.

**Jessa**: *REALLY don't think this is a good idea.*

I sigh and bite my nails.

**Me**: *Are you going to help me or not? I really wanna go cuz I've never been to a school dance.*

I wait several seconds for Jessa's reply, but there's nothing. Maybe she's busy so I text Trevor: *You got any dress up ideas for the dance?*

**Trevor**: *Is this your official ask? Don't I get candy or flowers?*

I snicker to myself.

**Me**: *No, this is it.*

**Trevor**: *Ok then. How about u be Storm?*

Ughhh, there goes that suggestion again.

**Me**: *No*

**Trevor**: *Catwoman? I bet a tight catsuit would be sexy on u*

I blush. Sexy? Me?

**Me**: *No*

Trevor sends a frown face. I try thinking of some superhero duos that haven't been overdone.

**Trevor**: *I don't know much about superheroes. Sorry.*

My time with my phone is dwindling. Who knows about superheroes? Xavier and JJ.

I text them both.

**Me to JJ and Xavier**: *Superhero suggestions? Be quick!*

**Xavier**: *How'd u get ur phone back?*

Good grief! I said be quick.

**Me**: *I have 5 minutes with my phone. Type fast.*

**Xavier**: *Thinking.*

**JJ:** *Why not be a real superhero, someone not fictional?*

**Me**: *That's a good idea. Examples?*

**JJ**: *Raven Wilkinson, Maya Angelou, Nina Simone, Harriet Tubman.*

**Me**: *All those sound great. But Harriet Tubman?? May be hard to dance in a long dress and coat. That's not hot.*

**Xavier**: *Actually you WILL be hot with all those clothes on!*

**JJ:** (,≥◡≤),

JJ sends a crying laughing anime-style emoticon. I swear my friends are so corny. In addition to being corny, they're nerds who prefer the typed out symbols of emoticons over emojis. I mean, who actually knows all those symbols?

**Xavier**: *Josephine Baker, she danced in banana leaves in France. She was topless though.*

I send a mad-face emoticon of my own; something JJ showed me: ☹_*Not helping, Xave.*

**JJ**: *You're creative enough to make anything work. Don't overthink it. Be original like only you can be.*

Best advice I've been given so far.

**Xavier:** (❤ω❤) *Yup. What J said.*

My time is up and I have to give my dad back my phone. Quickly, I text Trevor my idea.

**Trevor**: *But who can I be?*

**Me**: *Study your history and figure it out. Don't text me back. Have to give my phone to my dad.*

**Trevor**: *Ok.*

I give my phone back and then go to my room. Just as I remember that I probably should've turned my phone off, Dad enters my room while reading my phone. "Trevor says he'll pick you up at eight. Where y'all headed?"

Shoot! I told him not to text me back!

## Fifteen

# Resistance

"Not happenin'," My dad tells me.

I just finished explaining to my dad the reasons why I want to go to the school dance and why he should let me.

Reason #1: He can trust me.

Reason #2: I've been very responsible minus the whole nose piercing thing, but I still don't think that's a big deal.

Reason #3: I should be allowed to go because he went to dances when he was my age and so did Mama.

None of my reasons land. He stares at me with his chest puffed up like Superman. I don't think anyone has a father as strict as mine. In the past, I've hardly ever questioned him. A no, was a no. But not this time.

"Why can't I go to the dance?"

"I know what these young boys think they can get away with at dances."

"What can they get away with?" I ask honestly because I don't know.

He fidgets and rubs his head. "Well, for starters, I know that the dance starts at seven and this boy…Terrence—"

"Trevor, Dad. His name is Trevor."

Dad waves his hand. "Whatever. He's already starting off wrong by trying to pick you up an hour late. Second, there's the music that they play. It'll influence you, it'll make you feel things and if not you, then him and he'll try to…um…he'll…How old is this guy?"

I ignore his question because it's irrelevant if he's not going to let me attend.

Seeming uneasy, he shakes his head. "Look, you just can't go, alright?"

No, it's not alright. And that type of response is not good enough for me. Why deny me the part of high school that *is* high school?

"Did you go to dances?"

He smooths his hand around his goatee. His silence tells me everything I need to know.

Dad sits on my bed and takes a very deep breath. "Are you…are you sexually active?"

Where did that come from? How did we go from going to a dance to sex? Now I'm the one who's uncomfortable.

"No. I've never even had a boyfriend. But what does that have to do with this dance?"

"Sometimes guys think it's an expectation at the end of the night."

"But I don't have that expectation for myself. I just wanna dance. I'm not trying to get busy."

There will come a time where I *will* want to have sex, but that's not the case right now. My parents had given me the bare minimum on the birds and the bees talk, but now I wish they had told me more.

In fifth grade, there was "the talk" at school about what changes would start happening to our bodies. It was girls and boys combined so that the guys would know what we go through and the girls would know what the guys go through. Dad said that was different from how he grew up; they used to separate the boys and girls.

In middle school, there was Health Science where they talked about the male and female reproductive system. But even with that, there was nothing about the act of sex or what happens when you *want* to have sex with someone or someone wants to have sex with you. I knew about sexual assault, rape, venereal diseases, pregnancy prevention, condoms, birth control, and abstinence. But what about the basics? What about feelings and urges?

I knew plenty of girls who were having sex and others who started in middle school. They'd talk about it after class or in the locker room. It's how I know most of what I do know.

Jessa is a virgin as far as I know. Xavier is too—but he'd never confess that to anyone other than within our friend circle. JJ is definitely a virgin and has made it clear that he'd remain one until he meets his wife, or married his wife rather. If there were other virgins at our school, I didn't know about them because that's not something anyone would openly admit.

"*You* may not be trying to get busy but there are guys out there who are," Dad tells me.

"Not all guys are the same."

"True. Not all guys, but there are ways that…" Dad keeps trailing off and I don't understand. "I can't do this," he mumbles to himself. He walks out of my room, shutting the door behind him.

I go back to my work convinced that I'm going to the dance. Dad hadn't given me any good reason to believe that I shouldn't go.

## Sixteen

# T.G.I.F.

Waking up to look at the clock is pointless. Instead of lying in bed, I open my journal. The last time I wrote was Monday, March 27:

*In the dark, I search for you.*

I don't think I'm Nikki Giovanni or anything, but JJ had sort of been right about me writing poetry. It's like I step into another realm when I write. Most of my inspiration comes when we run in the mornings. It's funny that I can call myself a runner now. I've gotten better at it even though I only go on the weekends with JJ.

Spending time with him has been different, but in a good way. Like, in a way I didn't expect it to be. We'd hung out before but mostly with Jessa and Xavier. It's always been the four of us but lately, it's only been me, JJ and the sky. We don't need to talk; we know how to chill and just be.

With my pen ready to write, I realize I have so many thoughts traveling around in my mind that I don't know what to say first.

After about five minutes the page is filled with simple drawings of hearts and butterflies; my name and JJ's name written in various fonts. Holy cow! I didn't even realize I'd done this. It's like I stepped away from my mind or something. I rip out the page and throw it away.

* * *

After school, Jessa brings me home so she can critique my outfit for the dance next week.

"So glad it's Friday," she says, stretching across my bed. "One more week until we're out for spring break. After that, it'll be time to study for finals and then graduation, baby! Wooo!"

She's so pumped to be graduating that she counts down the days on her hand with an ink pen.

"Who are you going to prom with?" I ask. She'd told me a few guys had asked her but she hadn't said who she decided to go with.

Jessa props herself up by her elbows. "Soooo, don't make a big deal out of this, but I'm going with Xavier."

I make a big deal out of it. "What? Really? Are y'all together? I knew it. I knew it!"

Jessa holds up her hands to slow me down. "Clove, no, we're not together. Like for real, we're not."

My shoulders slump. She got me all worked up for nothin'. "Well, what's up with y'all then? Y'all argue like an old couple and now you tell me you're going to prom together. Sounds like you're in a relationship to me."

Jessa chews on her lip. She's been off lately. We don't talk like we used to. I thought it was because she was busy with Senior stuff but I'm beginning to think there's more to it than that.

"We *are* in a relationship," she says. "A friendship relationship. And friends can go to prom together, you know?"

"I know but—"

"Show me your outfit." She changes the subject.

Reaching in my closet, I take out a white button-up shirt, black tutu skirt that I made myself and some black leggings.

Jessa looks confused. "Uh, help me out here. What exactly are you supposed to be?"

I give her a hint. "The only thing I need are black boots and red suspenders."

She thinks for a second, but I can tell she's still clueless.

"Jess, I'm going to be a firefighter."

"Ohhhhh. Wow, you're going to be one hot firefighter."

"Thanks."

"No, I mean you're really going to be hot. You're gonna burn up in those black fleece leggings. Go without the leggings and show off those legs, girl."

"No way. My dad won't go for that. Besides, my tutu is too short for bare legs. Maybe I can get a different pair of leggings or some tights. And I need some red suspenders too. Can you take me to go get some?"

Jessa shakes her head. "I would but I have somewhere to be in about ten minutes. But you should text JJ, you know his mama always has stuff like that. "

Jessa's right. Mrs. Jourdan is our church arts coordinator. She has a collection of props and costumes for plays.

As Jessa waves goodbye, I press JJ's picture on my phone.

"Hey," he answers. "Didn't I see you an hour ago? Aren't you tired of me?"

"Tired of you? I could never. Do you have red suspenders?" I ask him.

"Mmm, I don't but my mom might. I can ask her for you."

"Great. Thanks. Also, do you wanna meet me in the morning to watch the sun rise again?"

"Of course I do. Meet you at the stop sign?"

"Yep."

"Okay, cool."

"Cool."

I'm still holding the phone. I want to say something but I'm feeling unsure about it.

"Clove?"

"Yeah."

"Is there anything else?"

There is but there isn't. "Um, so, are you still going to the dance with Tisha?"

"I think so."

Oh. I was hoping that would change. I still don't understand why. What does he see in her?

"Are you still going with Trevor?"

I roll over on my bed, crossing my ankle over my knee. "I don't know. We have nothing in common. Talking to him is…" *Not as exciting as talking to you*, I want to tell him. "I don't know. It's like he's just cute and that's it."

JJ's quiet.

"You still there?" I ask him.

"Yes. So, what are you going to do?"

I have to think about it. Trevor invited me to a house party tonight. I don't know much about house parties, but I've heard they can be chill or exactly the opposite. If Dad were in town, I'd have to explain to him where I was going, but he's not. In fact, he'd been so busy flying in and out of town that talking to me hasn't been on his radar. We hadn't even finished the last conversation we tried to have about me going to the dance. As far as I know, I'm going. And I think I might go to this party tonight too.

"Trevor invited us to a party tonight. Wanna go?" I ask JJ.

Seconds of silence tick by. "Um, he invited *us*? As in—"

"Me, you, Jessa, and Xavier."

Gram is more likely to let me go out tonight if she knows all of my friends are going. Plus, I think Gram has a bowling league tournament. I like that she keeps fit for her age but it'll be far too boring for me to sit and watch. I figure since she's going out I should go out too.

"House parties aren't something I get into, *tu sais?*" JJ says mixing in French again.

I should've known he wouldn't be down to go. I'm about to tell him nevermind but then he says, "What time should I pick you up?"

# Seventeen

## *House Party*

At 7:51 p.m. JJ is at my door. I told him the party started at 8:30. He's early.

"Sup, chump!" I tease.

He eyes me up and down quickly, making me notice my plaid button-up shirt isn't buttoned up quite right. One side is longer than the other.

"Hold on a sec," I shut the door and fix my buttons. When I open the door again, JJ has a smirk on his face.

"Thought my little brother was the only one who buttoned his shirts wrong."

"Shuddup."

Xavier and a disgruntled Jessa sit in the backseat of Mr. Jourdan's old Audi. Less than thirty minutes ago, me and Jessa got into a small argument.

"Clove, I don't think this thing with you and Trevor is a good idea." Jessa said over the phone. "There are better fish in the sea."

I rolled my eyes. "You sound like your dad. Fish in the sea?"

"You know what I mean. I've heard things about him.'

"I've heard things about a lot of people, including you." After I said that last part I knew I shouldn't have.

"What have you heard?" she asked.

I wanted to change the subject, I *needed* to change the subject because what I'd heard wasn't something I wanted to say aloud.

"Fine, Jess. Don't go with us. It'll just be me, JJ and maybe Xavier. I'll call you after."

Jessa has serious FOMO and once I told her not to go, she wanted to go. I was glad she'd dropped the subject about what I'd heard.

Xavier and JJ talk about something I could care less about. I don't want them eavesdropping into our conversation so I text Jessa as they talk.

**Me**: *Can u please be cool?*

**Jessa**: *I'm cool. But you're making a really bad choice.*

**Me**: *What happened with u and Trevor?*

**Jessa**: *Nothing.*

**Me**: *Lies you tell.*

**Jessa**: *I just don't think u should go out with him. And this party...big mistake.*

**Me**: *It's at Hannah's house. She likes JJ and she is super kind.*

When Trevor had given me the address, I recognized it immediately as Hannah Hopper's home. She has one of those big mansion-type houses. We'd been there plenty of times for youth group meetings.

**Jessa**: *Ask yourself, why would a girl like Hannah throw a house party that includes Trevor????*

I had asked myself that. It'd definitely surprised me that Hannah was throwing a party that Trevor knew about.

**Me**: *Maybe he meant it's a church party and he's trying to get to know me better.*

**Jessa**: *U don't really believe that.*

For once, I had tried not to overthink it. But maybe thinking about it was something I should've done.

"What's the address again?" JJ asks.

I scroll through my phone and find Trevor's message. "5244 Cherrydrop Lane"

"Gate Code?"

"Pound Pound, 3069."

"Hmmm, those numbers do not sound right. That's not Hannah's gate code, is it?"

I don't really remember. It's been such a long time since I've been out here. After JJ punches in the code, we drive through the gates and onto a tree-lined street. We pass by huge homes with golf-course sized yards.

"There it is right there," I say pointing to Hannah's house.

JJ passes right by it. "That is not 5244, that's 5422."

Oh. Whoops. Jessa was right. It was foolish of me to think we were going to Hannah's house.

Once we reach our destination, the street is so packed that finding a space close to the party isn't an option. It takes us a few minutes to walk down the block. As we do, we pass by a car that's fogged up and moving. Since we all know what they're doing, we keep our eyes straight ahead.

The closer we get, the louder the music. When we finally arrive at the party house, the yard is trashed with red cups. People stand outside talking and laughing. The strong scent of alcohol hits me and I hesitate to step further inside. It's like my nose is warning me, stopping me dead in my tracks.

"You sure you wanna do this?" Xavier asks.

My stomach does a flip and bile rises in my throat. It's safe to say my body is telling me no. But this is all part of the adventurous girl I said I wanted to be. I'm walking on the wild side; the dangerous side. Fear is not welcomed here.

What does welcome me is a big cloud of smoke that I inhale from the porch. I begin coughing, choking from the smoke.

To my surprise, it's Trevor that's outside smoking. "Dang, girl! You a'ight? Wasn't sure you were coming."

My friends pat my back like I'm a baby, trying to help me clear the smoke from my lungs. Finally, I get myself together enough to speak. "I'm good," I say, hoarsely.

I make my nose and stomach pretend that everything is fine. Just because other people are drinking and smoking, doesn't mean I have to. Trevor takes my hand and leads me into the house. I'm so stoked about him holding my hand that I don't pay attention to if my friends have followed us inside.

Trevor asks me something but the music is so loud that I can barely hear what he said.

"I SAID DO YOU WANT A DRINK?"

I shake my head no. Trevor pushes through people who already seem drunk. Those that aren't drunk are either kissing or grinding to the music. Behind me, Jessa grabs my hand, letting me know she's with me even though I have no clue where the boys went. We make our way through the crowd into the kitchen where the music is somewhat subdued enough where we won't have to scream to talk. Two girls are leaning against a marble counter making out with each other.

I avert my eyes and notice Trevor staring at them. He pours me a soda, handing it to me while continuing to ogle the girls.

I snap my fingers in his face. "Sorry," he says, bringing his attention back to me. "You can't fault me for looking right?"

I narrow my eyes at him. "Actually, yeah I can. And I told you I didn't want a drink."

"Chill. It's soda. Thought you meant you didn't want a *drink* drink. Like alcohol."

With a grimace, I put down the cup. Jessa's still holding my hand but she's watching the girls.

Trevor smirks at her. "You thinking of joining them?" That should've been my moment to defend her, but it was related to the rumors I'd heard and I wanted to hear her response.

Jessa releases my hand. "Clove, I will be wherever he isn't."

She leaves and I don't go after her like I should. Instead, I turn back to Trevor. Even though I didn't want anything to drink, I take a sip of the orange bubbly liquid hoping that carbonation will ease the queasiness in my stomach.

"Wanna go somewhere else?" Trevor asks me. I scan the house for JJ and Xavier, but don't see them.

I nod. "Sure. But who's house is this?"

Trevor takes my hand again, pulling me towards some stairs. "A friend of mine."

What friend does he know that lives in a house like this? The architecture is beautiful. I can only guess the parents who own this residence are out of town. There's no way I'd let all these people trash something so elegant.

Trevor turns down a hallway that has almost all of its doors shut. He finds an open one and leads me inside. It's much, much quieter here. Now we can talk and get to know each other.

* * *

I come out of the room quickly, smoothing my hands over my hair to make sure it's still in place. The party seems wilder than it did when I arrived. People are all over the steps and the smell of weed is even stronger.

I plant my feet on each step carefully so as to not disturb the couples kissing and talking. Once I'm down the steps, I find Jessa in the kitchen talking to some girl with a soda can in her hand. When she sees me, she stops talking and takes me by the wrist.

"Clove, tell me you weren't off somewhere alone with Trevor?"

I don't wanna lie, so I say nothing and for once I actually feel like sobbing.

She gives me a once-over. "Noooo." The way she said *no* was as if someone died. Before I can say anything to quell what she might be thinking, Xavier and JJ find us. They look at me in the same way Jessa just did. My shame is written all over my face and I am most definitely ready to go.

"Everything okay?" Xavier asks.

It's not but I don't want to talk about it. "Yeah. Let's go."

Xavier leads the way through the patio where there are even more people in a pool.

Jessa pulls me by my wrist while Xavier and JJ continue walking ahead of us. "Clove," she whispers.

"Fix your buttons."

I look down. They're incorrectly buttoned…again.

# Eighteen

# Golden Hour

As soon as I wake up, I text JJ to tell him I don't want to go running anymore. I don't want to see the judgmental look he'll have on his face after last night. What was I thinking going to that party?

Last night the ride home was quiet and awkward. Once I got home, JJ opened my car door. Not necessarily out of chivalry, but because his dad's car door was jammed from the inside. He walked me to the front door and adjusted the collar of my shirt for me. It wasn't until I got inside the bathroom that I realized he was trying to help me cover up my most visible mistake: a hickey branded on my neck like the *Scarlet Letter*.

When Trevor took me to the room, I thought he wanted to talk, but I was naive—very naive. We talked for only a minute and then he started kissing my neck. Caught between pleasure and confusion, I let him continue. My instincts didn't kick in to tell me that this was not the right person for me to be with until after all of my buttons were undone.

"No, sorry. This isn't right," I said.

Trevor licked his lips while staring at my body, the parts of me no one had ever seen. I barely knew Trevor and we hardly talked on the phone. If I was going to let anyone see me, it needed to be someone who loved me naked or not. And Trevor just wasn't it. He didn't deserve to see me. Unfortunately, I came to that conclusion much too late.

He rubbed his chin. "It's cool. I saw what I wanted to see."

Hearing that statement made my stomach turn sour. I fled the room as quickly as possible.

There's a light tap on my window. JJ is on the other side. He must not have gotten my message. I lift the window. "Guess you didn't get my text."

"I got it. *Allons-y*," he says.

I think he misunderstood what I said or maybe I didn't understand the French correctly but I always thought *Allons-y* meant "Let's go."

"I don't wanna go anymore."

"Why?"

I know why, but I don't want to say it aloud. JJ gives me a minute to reply, but when I don't, he says, "It's forty-five degrees and I'm here outside your window at 5:30 in the morning. Let's go."

The assertiveness in his tone stupefies me. He's never been this firm with me before. Perhaps I should explain why I think I shouldn't go.

"JJ, about last night—"

"No," he cuts me off.

*No?* "But I want to expla-"

"Don't."

He scrolls through his phone and then my phone chimes. He's sent me his run playlist and vanishes before I can finish reading all the artists and songs on the list. Another message appears on my phone.

**JJ**: *Get dressed. I'll be on your front porch.*

Dang! For some reason his self-confidence and attitude is working for me. I do as he requests, getting dressed as fast as I can all while sneezing.

As soon as I step onto the porch, JJ starts jogging. Geez, can I get a warm-up walk?

I catch up to him, our rhythm matching the beat of the music. If I wasn't so busy trying to keep up with JJ, I might actually stop and dance to the songs.

As my feet hit the pavement, I admire the sky that's already periwinkle, the stars less visible. I try to recall all the different twilights JJ told me about, but

I can't quite remember them in the right order.

Sooner than expected, we're back at the hill. At first, I rest my hands on my knees but immediately stand up when I remember what JJ told me about breathing.

"Which twilight is this again?" I say, trying to catch my breath.

"Civil. Also known as dawn." He takes a sports bottle and squirts water into his mouth. Then he hands it to me. I take in as much water as I can while still saving him plenty.

Once we reach the top of the hill, I collapse against the tree that still has no leaves. I give my breath a few minutes to steady and then I ask, "Why do you think God keeps waking me up at this time?"

JJ stares out at the horizon. "What makes you think it's God?"

Ever since we were younger he'd often turn questions around to make me think about things for myself. I had asked myself this question many times and I wasn't really sure of the answer.

"By now," JJ says. "It could be that your body is used to waking up at this time. Perhaps it's your circadian rhythm."

I don't truly think that's what he believes.

As the sun rises, the sky turns into this beautiful gold hue. Gold. Gold birthday. I started waking up like this the day before my Golden Birthday, the day of my birthday and the day after. I've been waking up before the break of dawn ever since.

"This time of day," JJ says quietly. "Is known as the golden hour. It happens at sunset too. It's the moment when the sun appears to give gold light. It's a photographer's best time to take a photo because everything is just right; the lighting, the atmosphere, and the stillness. They all provoke solitude and meditation. We've watched this together a few times now. I think you know why you're waking up at this time."

Once again, he's right. If I quit avoiding the obvious, I do know. My mom and dad used to get up at five faithfully to read and pray together. I think I'm supposed to be doing the same.

"No one our age gets up at this time to read their Bible and pray," I say.

"How do you know? I'm up."

True. But I was convinced it was so he could run and lately, so he could run with me.

"JJ, the playlist you sent me was really good but…I think I'm done with God."

"Okay." Is all he says.

We lay on our backs in the cool grass and bask in the light. The sun gives so much warmth that it feels like a kiss.

I turn my head towards him. "Why'd you make me come out here with you this morning even when I told you I didn't want to?"

JJ puts his hands behind his head. I'm tempted to lay my head on his chest but instead focus on the cookie crumb freckles on his nose and cheeks.

"I didn't *make* you. I can't make you do anything. You did it on your own," JJ says.

"But you were bossy. You told me to get dressed and that'd you be on my porch. I didn't want to leave you out there."

JJ rolls onto his side so he can face me. His eyes peer into mine. "So you're saying you did this for me? You got out of bed, got dressed, *maybe* brushed your teeth and ran up this hill all for me?"

He waits for my answer with a face so serious that it makes me question my motive. Did I do this for him? No, I did this for me. I needed the run, needed to feel the wind in my face, needed the sun to kiss me in only a way it can. And if I'm honest, I wanted this time with JJ.

Before I can reply, he says, "You did brush your teeth, right?"

I roll my eyes. "Yes, you dork. Did you brush yours?"

"Always."

He sits up and wraps his arms around his knees. "I'm not giving up on you, Clove. Even if you want to give up on yourself. I'm going to push and pull you out of the dark and into the sunlight."

All the things he's saying to me and the way he's saying them, he's never done before. He begins to get up and extends his hand so he can help me up. We run all the way back to my neighborhood. When I want to stop and take a break, JJ encourages me.

*Keep going.*

*Come on.*

*You can do this.*

*Breathe.*

*You're doing wonderful.*

He says these things over and over until I start saying them to myself. I don't stop running until we turn onto my street. I breathe hard, with my hands on top of my head.

"See, you did good even though you didn't want to. Up top." JJ puts his hand up for me to slap him a high-five but my high-five is weak compared to the five he gives.

"Once you start doing this consistently, it'll get better."

I don't know if I believe him or if I even want to be consistent with this. Using my spare key, I unlock the front door. "Wanna come in? I can make us something to eat."

"Does it involve you cooking?"

I push the door open. "No, it involves cereal, milk, and a spoon."

He thinks for a moment. "You know, I actually have to do some weight lifting down at Xave's. Wanna weight lift?"

What a silly question. I don't want to lift weights. I want water, breakfast, and sleep. In that order.

"I'll help you lift and then we'll get Xavier to take us back to my house," JJ says. "We can have breakfast there."

That does sound like a better idea. My house is empty because dad's still out of town and Gram went back home after she stopped by to check on me last night. She wasn't even here when I got in. It's kind of funny that a sixty-something year old lady has a social life better than mine.

Taking JJ up on his offer, we walk side by side to Xavier's house.

"Are you sure he's up?"

"Yes, he's up. He gets up early as well." He looks at me with an expression that says I'm supposed to know what that means. And in a way I do but it's hard to believe both of them get up early to pray or read the Bible.

For the first three minutes or so I watch Xavier and JJ take turns bench pressing. Then it's my turn. I definitely don't want to bench press anything.

Xavier begins taking off the heavy weights for me.

"No," I say. "What makes you think I can't lift what y'all lift? I can handle the weight."

Xavier and JJ exchange glances, then Xavier slides the weights back on.

I sit on the bench and lay back. Xavier stands above my head. "Ready when you are, Princess."

"Don't call me princess, Xave."

"Fine then. Lift."

I push and push and push. Nothing happens. Isn't he supposed to help me or something?

"You're not helping. You helped JJ."

"The heavy lifting was all him. I only spotted him, making sure he didn't drop it in case it got to be too much. How about we start with smaller weights, eh?"

"No, I don't want the smaller weights." Frustrated, I sit up.

JJ squats down in front of me. "Clove, you have to start small. Small steps equal big change."

Why is he all philosophical today? Fine. I take the smaller weights. This time JJ spots me.

We do about three rounds of bench pressing, followed by push-ups, and lastly pull-ups. I don't even try to do what the guys do. For the pull-ups, I hang onto the bar.

"Hang in there," Xavier jokes.

"Lame!" I say and then the three of us start laughing.

After we finish, I'm all sweaty. Rather than go to JJ's house for breakfast like we'd planned, I decide to go home so I can shower.

As JJ walks me back home, he says, "So, no breakfast? I had a green protein smoothie all planned out for you."

*Yuck.* "Sounds delicious," I say flatly. "But I think I better shower first. Maybe we can meet up later?"

Truthfully, I don't want this time with him to end. His hair is wet around the edges and his cheeks are flush from working out. I'm very tempted to touch his face regardless of how sticky it might be. He makes my heart race and there are butterflies flying everywhere in my stomach. Lately, whenever we hang out, he gives me these feelings. This is how I should've felt last night. But Trevor gave me no butterflies.

"Spending the entire day with you would be awesome," JJ says.

"But?" I prod. I can tell that there's a rebuttal coming. He must be busy, have a date with Tisha or something.

"But," he echoes. "I have a project to finish and my mom wants me to help clean-up. We have company coming over for the weekend. If I'm not mistaken, I think you're going to be hanging out with my mom later tonight."

My eyes widen. This was the first time I was hearing about it. Where are we going? What are we doing? Why am I just now finding out? All these questions must be written on my face, because JJ says,"You have questions and I don't have all the answers. My mom will call you later, okay?"

"Okay."

JJ begins to back away, watching me as he does. Not knowing what else to do, I wave goofily. It feels like a magnetic force is between us. The farther he gets, the stronger the pull. He must have magnets in his soul.

# Nineteen


*Karaoke*

When JJ said I was going out with his mom, I wasn't expecting to be standing on stage in front of a smoke-filled room, with a bar, and a touch screen jukebox that plays karaoke. I don't even know how I mustered the courage to get up here.

Mrs. Jourdan, a guy named Sian, another one named Crane, and a woman named Mya sit at a bar- top table in front, smiling and cheering me on. When Mrs. Jourdan told me that her friends were in town, I didn't realize she meant Mama's friends too. I know them, and they've known me since I was little. They'd all been at the funeral, but I was too out of it to remember.

I listened while they exchanged stories about my mom. They talked about how she was never afraid of anything. For a split second I thought I could be courageous too. Which is why I decided to sing a Karaoke song. Now that I'm up here, I realize I'm not that courageous. It takes guts to sing in front of a crowd of people but I seriously think my guts might spill all over the floor.

When Mrs. Jourdan sang, she got a standing ovation. I didn't know she had such a beautiful voice. Mya went next. Her voice wasn't great but people still clapped.

The room is dim and all I can see is the glow of orange wristbands worn by the 21 and up crowd. I wipe my sweaty palms on my pants and wait for the music to begin. I try to give myself an internal pep talk. *I'm brave. I can do this. If I can get my nose pierced, then this is a piece of cake.*

The song is upbeat but old school, one of my mom's favorite artists: Whitney Houston. I start dancing to calm my nerves. The words turn yellow which I think means I'm supposed to sing. My voice comes out all wrong but Mrs. Jourdan and her friends cheer me on. One of them holds up a lit flame from a lighter. The other shines his phone screen in the air. Their antics make me laugh, causing me to fall behind on the lyrics.

Mrs. Jourdan cups her hands around her mouth."You got this, Dearest!"

I sound awful, like a turkey gobbling and warbling. Oh goodness this is terrible. But I sing the chorus with more confidence because that's about the only part I know. It's also the part of the song I can relate to; wanting to dance with someone who loves me or maybe even just likes me.

I have a rush of energy inside making me dance even more as I get into the song.

When the music stops, everyone claps, including the people at the bar. I know I probably sounded like a wet cat meowing at the moon, but I appreciate the enthusiasm.

Mrs. Jourdan hugs me. "You did so good!"

She can't possibly mean that.

Mya puts her drink in the air. "Cheers to courage!" We clink glasses and then Sian asks how I feel.

I'm out of breath like I've gone for another run. "Pretty good," I say. "It was scary but exciting at the same time."

Mya nudges Mrs. Jourdan's arm. "You should've brought Jonah. This would've been perfect for getting him to combat his shyness."

If JJ were here, I definitely would not have gotten up and sang that song the way I did—or at all for that matter.

"Clove, have you ever heard Jonah sing?" Mrs. Jourdan asks.

That's silly. JJ can't sing. "No, ma'am."

"He's got a beautiful voice and I'm not just saying that because I'm his mom."

That's just preposterous. Next I suppose she'll tell me he can dance too.

I've never seen him do either one of these things.

"He does have a good voice," Crane affirms. "Is he still thinking of going to Vanderbilt?"

Mrs. Jourdan talks to them while I try to envision JJ singing, but I can't. If what Mrs. Jourdan says is true, then JJ is more multifaceted than I ever knew. He's like a Boy Wonder, both smart and talented.

## Twenty

# *Liked or Loved*

It's after 10 p.m. before Mrs. Jourdan and I get back on the road. I listened to her friends talk about high school and growing up in Smalltown. Mrs. Jourdan wasn't born and raised here, but came from Louisiana while in high school. Following graduation, she studied in France which is where she met Mr. Jourdan. I knew all of this from JJ, but Mrs. Jourdan gave me the backstory anyway.

Mrs. Jourdan yawns and then says. "Did you have fun?"

"Yes ma'am. Thank you."

"Oh don't thank me, Dearest. It was my pleasure. However, I wasn't talking about Karaoke. Did you have fun at the party last night?"

My eyes bulge. I swear JJ tells his parents everything, but not in a snitch type of way. He's just super open with them. I'm almost positive he didn't tell her *everything*. I don't know if I should answer.

"You know, Clove," Mrs. Jourdan begins again. "I know you have your Gram, but if you ever want to talk, I want you to call me, alright?"

"Yes ma'am." A few questions come to mind, but I go with the first one that sticks out most.

"Was there ever a time you thought about dating one of your friends? Like, when y'all were going to school together?"

She ponders my question. "Mmmmm, not really. We've all pretty much always been friends. Mya and Sian dated for a little bit but soon realized that it just wasn't right for them. Thankfully, they hadn't gotten in too deep and it didn't ruin the friendship."

Grateful that she didn't ask why I asked that question, I change the subject.

"My dad doesn't want me to go to the dance and I don't understand why. He went to dances when he was my age. He got to go to movies with girls and date and stuff. Why won't he let me do these things?"

Mrs. Jourdan stops at a red light. "Your father is doing what dads sometimes do. You're young, smart, and pretty. He wants to protect you from everything, but you're both learning that's not possible. No one can protect everyone from everything. I can tell you do's and don'ts but either you'll heed them or experience them."

I know what she means. Jessa had warned me not to hang out with Trevor but I chose experience as a lesson and it sucked. Apparently, it sucked way too hard because I feel like I have the mark of the beast on my neck. Mrs. Jourdan said nothing about the scarf I chose to wear tonight even though it's warm.

"How will I know if I've met the right person?" I ask.

She smiles slightly. "What *right* person are you looking for? You want someone to love you or like you? Hook up with or be friends with?"

I'm not sure that I'm looking for either of those things. But I understand that my usage of the word "right" wasn't right. Without waiting for my response to my questions, she says, "The *right* person will push you to be your best self and bring out all the good in you that you didn't even know you had. The person that truly loves you will know your value and your worth. They respect you and your body. Does that make sense?"

That clears up quite a few things for me. "Yes ma'am." I say quietly.

If it wasn't clear last night that Trevor is not the person for me, it's crystal clear now. If I'm honest with myself, I knew where he was leading me when he took my hand but I didn't say anything. And when he patted the space beside him on the bed, warning signals shot off everywhere, but I ignored them. When he went straight for my neck while simultaneously unbuttoning my shirt, I still said nothing. There were mixed sensations that I was feeling; agitation, fear, pleasure and needing to feel wanted. Before Trevor's hand could reach the button on my jeans, I pushed him away.

"I don't wanna do this," I said.

"Really?" he asked. "I thought you were down."

I shook my head. "No, not like this. This isn't right."

"It's right for me," Trevor said.

"Don't you want us to get to know each other better?" I asked.

He went for my neck again. "*I'm trying* to get to know you better."

Again, I pushed him away. "No, that's not what I mean. Can we just talk?"

Trevor blinked at me in disbelief. "*Now* you wanna talk? You barely say anything to me. Thought you just wanted to hook up."

I couldn't believe that was the impression he got from me. Just because I didn't talk much didn't mean I wanted to fool around instead.

"Why you even wanna go to the dance with me if you ain't gon' let me smash?" he asked.

I hated the word "smash." I wasn't some fruit or cake that could be crumbled. The fact that he even used that word was a turn off in itself. When I do have sex, it has to be for love, with love and out of love. I felt so stupid. I hadn't made up my mind about what I wanted until that very moment and it was all so late.

I quickly buttoned my shirt. "You know what," I said. "I shoulda known you were trash. You weren't trying very hard to get to know me either."

"Actually, I was," Trevor leered at me like I was a snack.

I shuddered in disgust and wished I could press rewind. "The parts of me you were trying to get to know will never ever be in your view again."

He rubbed his chin with a smile. "I saw what I wanted to see. We're good."

Someone knocked on the door. "Come in," Trevor said. Mars waltzed in with a red cup in her hand. She acted as though she didn't see me and started talking to Trevor in code. It was full of acronyms and terminology that I didn't understand. Before I could leave the room, they were all over each other.

"Mrs. Jourdan—" I begin.

She cuts me off and taps my knee. "Just call me Mama Jourdan."

"Mama Jourdan, what if I've found a person like you've described, but... but..."

I can't talk to her about her son, can I? It'd be obvious who I was talking about, because out of all of my friends, I've spent the most time with JJ.

Mama Jourdan hums as she drives, then she asks, "What do you know about this Tisha girl Jonah's going to the dance with?"

She's awful. That's what I want to say, but I try to think of something nice or positive to say about Tisha.

"We've known her since elementary," I finally say.

Mama Jourdan waits for me to tell her more. "That's all you got for me? Jonah brought her over one time but she was acting fake. Moms can see right through that mess. She's pretty but I need to know what else. Keep it real with me, Clove."

I forgo the nice talk and tell her what I know about Tisha and everything she's ever done to me. "I don't know why JJ wants to go with Tisha. He's too good for her. She's all nasty and mean and he's good-hearted, honest, kind, funny, compassionate, caring, and he's highly intelligent. I feel like I can talk to JJ about anything. He volunteers random information daily and it's so nerdy that all I can do is laugh. And he always knows when or when not to talk, sometimes it's like he's in my head and—"

I stop myself because I'm rambling. If my mission was to keep my feelings for JJ a secret, I'd failed. My cheeks feel warm as I twirl my hair between my fingers.

"Hmmmmm," Mama Jourdan says with a smile spreading across her face. "Sounds like he's going to the dance with the wrong girl."

# Twenty-One

## The Test

It's the Monday before Spring break and everybody is anxious to get through the week. However, I can't help but feel like people are staring at me as I walk down the hall. Or maybe I'm imagining it.

Trevor walks by me with his boys. They all undress me with their eyes. One of them licks their lips and says, "I like your udders." Then they all laugh and continue down the hall.

Udders? It only takes two seconds for me to figure out what they mean: Trevor did a kiss and tell.

Jessa stands next to me, with her face as red as a beet. She seems to be embarrassed *for* me. "Clove, I hate to say I told you so, but I told you."

Doesn't sound like she hated to say that at all. I run into the girls bathroom. Just like my first day back after Mama died, I go into the biggest stall and put my hands to my face, silently scolding myself for being so stupid.

Giggling voices enter the bathroom.

"Oh my gawd, I heard she's black and white all over. A real cow!" Tisha's voice says. "I'll be so glad when I pass Mr. T's test so I can stop pretending to like her."

"What about Jonah?" Mars asks her. "Are you still going to the dance with him?"

"Nope. Just need his answers for the test. We'll sit next to each other. I'll get the answers and be done."

"That's a shame," Mar says. 'Jonah's such a good guy. Geeky, but good."

"Then you date him," Tisha tells her. "He bores me. Always talking about random scientific stuff like stars, animals, weather patterns and crap. I'm so done pretending to be interested. He's got the highest GPA in our class, all I need is his brain."

I cover my mouth to keep from gasping out loud. My heart aches for Jonah. I knew Tisha was up to something, but I hadn't been sure of exactly what it was until now.

***

Trevor doesn't sit with us at lunch, but Tisha remains at our table and sits close to JJ, borrowing his notes for today's test. With all the fake studying she's done, she could probably pass the test on her own.

She gives me a fake smile. "OMG, Clove, I love your hair today. What products do you use?"

I don't know how to respond because I'm thinking about how to tell JJ about Tisha before our class starts.

Trevor's ex-girlfriend, Christa, walks by me. "Hey, Clove."

I don't get the chance to say anything, because I feel something cold on my head. It runs down my face and smells like chocolate milk. Shivering, I open my mouth in shock and catch the look of horror on both JJ and Xavier's face. Both of them are stuck in their seats not knowing what to do while Tisha bursts into laughter.

I've had enough. Instantly, I'm up from the table, shoving Trevor's ex toward the trash can. She loses her balance and falls straight inside the can. I had expected more of a fight but she's stuck, so I turn to Tisha who's laughing like a hyena. One glance at her tray of uneaten mashed potatoes and I know just what they should be mashed into.

I flip the tray into her face. The mashed potatoes are so thick they make the tray stick to her face for a second. It brings me satisfaction. JJ and Xavier's chins are so low they might as well be on the table.

Someone pulls my hair from behind, sending shots of pain through my scalp. I've never been in a fight, but it's on now.

I reach behind me and grab a fist full of what feels like Christa's hair and yank. To my horror, her hair is in my hands. All of it hangs loosely from my fingers. I almost freak out until I realize it's a lace front wig.

Christa's head is covered by a stocking cap with cornrows showing underneath. Her mood quickly shifts from humiliation to anger. I give her back her wig. I'm mad and in the middle of a fight, but I didn't want the girl to be bald. Before Christa can reach for it, someone pushes me from behind and I land on top of Christa. We tumble onto the floor.

Tisha knocks me off of Christa and misses a punch to my face. With the wig still in my hands, I slap her across the face. She lands a wayward jab right where my nose ring is. I scream in pain, flail my legs, and shove her head back with the wig in her face. Kicks, punches, and hair pulling is all happening at once. I don't know if I'm fighting one, two, or three people, but I'm in pain.

Someone blows a whistle and I'm being lifted and pulled away. I can now see that I was indeed fighting three girls: Tisha, Mars, and Christa.

***

Dad's not happy when he picks me up from school early. I was planning to give him the details as soon as my nose and head stopped hurting but he hasn't given me a chance. He's been talking to himself, to me, and to God nonstop.

"What am I doing wrong here?" Dad asks, driving with two hands firmly on the steering wheel. "If you know, please tell me. I'm lost. A fight? You got in a fight with three girls? You pushed one in a trash can and then beat her with her own wig, threw food in another girl's face, and what was up with the third one? Did she just jump in for the fun of it all?"

It all sounds kind of funny when he says it like that. Christa's wig has got to be a tangled mess by now. I start chuckling but then it goes into a full-blown, uncontrollable laugh.

"This isn't funny, Clove."

I try to stop laughing but can't.

Dad gets angry. "Have you lost your mind!"

Yep. I think I've finally come undone. I envision myself searching a field for my brain, wandering aimlessly. This thought makes me burst out laughing all over again. It's all I know to do right now. In my mind, I've created a list of all the things that have gone away from me.

Skin pigment. *Check.*

Mom. *Check.*

Dignity. *Check*

Friends. *Check*

Mind. *Check.*

Nose ring…I touch my nose and wince from the pain. It's still there. *Whew.*

Dad pulls into our driveway. "Start by telling me what happened. How did the fight start?"

I think about it but don't know where to begin. If I tell him how Tisha only wanted JJ to cheat off his paper it would seem like I was fighting for JJ. That'll cause a whole different conversation.

"Christa poured chocolate milk over my head so I pushed her. I didn't mean for her to fall in the trash can. Then she got out of the trash can and pulled my hair. So I pulled her hair. I didn't know it would come off. I thought everybody who wore lace fronts knew to use glue and or bobby pins."

Dad rubs a hand over his mustache several times and it seems like he's trying to cover a smile. He's gotta admit this is pretty funny. I continue on with my story but leave out Trevor having anything to do with any of it.

"Then Tisha started a rumor about me that wasn't true so I smashed mashed potatoes into her face. She got mad at that so her and her friend came after me. I had to fight, Dad. I had to. It's like David and Goliath."

Dad brings his hand up. "Don't do that. Don't try to bring the Bible into this. 'Cause if you were thinking about the Bible you'd know that anger lodges in the hearts of fools. Ecclesiastes 7:9. As for Goliath, God is bigger than any giant. You'd know that if you quit skippin' church."

"Yeah, well everybody out here doesn't know the Bible," I say. "Everybody doesn't believe in the kindness and goodness of God. So why should I? I been going to church praisin' God for what? So some idiot can drive right

109

into my Mama!"

I get out of the car and slam the door.

"Hey! Don't slam my door!"

He cares way too much about his precious, classic car. I turn and scream two words that I immediately regret. The impact of my words register on his face as hurt then anger. His hand raises up to strike me and I brace myself for the impact.

But it doesn't come. I open one eye and see his hand held in mid-air. It stays there for a few seconds before going to his side slowly. "Clove, you need to leave," he says.

I don't think I heard him correctly so I blink several times as if that helps me hear.

"You need to leave," he says again.

"What? Why? Where am I going?"

The first words out of my mouth should've been "I'm sorry," but they weren't. At this moment I don't feel like apologizing, especially now that he's kicking me out of the house.

"You're not going on the college tour. If I can't trust you in town, how am I going to trust you out of town?" My dad says through gritted teeth. "Pack a bag and get out."

# Twenty-Two

## Foresight

Dad made me wait outside while Gram picked me up from my house. "Your dad just needs some time to cool off," she says. "I'm sure he'll still let you go on the college tour. It's educational and I know he wants you to see all the campuses so you can pick a school."

Gram keeps talking, but I stare out the window, watching rain fall. I used to like rainy days because they were great for sitting by a fire and reading a book. Now it's like the weather tries to mirror my life, feeding into my pain. It's dark, dreary, and depressing.

Once I'm at Gram's house, I lay on her bed and fall asleep. When I wake up, it's dark outside and my head is pounding at my temples and even at the scalp. The house is eerily quiet and I can only assume that Gram went out again.

I need medicine, pain killers, something strong because obviously what I took earlier didn't work. I hunt through my overnight bag for the pills I thought I'd packed but they're not there. Dang it!

The doorbell rings, sounding like thunder in my head. I open the door to a bruised-faced, split-lipped JJ. What on earth? Did he get in a fight?

Taking his hand, I immediately bring him into the kitchen where I take bags of frozen vegetables out of the freezer. I wrap a bag of corn in a towel and hold it against his jaw. He takes a bag of peas and holds it against my chin.

"JJ, what'd you get yourself into?" I whisper. I don't know why I'm whispering, perhaps it's because we're so close and he probably has a headache like I do.

He looks me in the eyes but doesn't answer, only continues to hold the bag of frozen vegetables to my face, allowing me to do the same for him. I feel like kissing him so I put the veggies down and move my lips towards his.

"Clove, no. Not like this," he whispers.

I don't understand. What does he mean not like this? Am I not good enough? Does he not feel what I feel? He has to.

"Not like this… not like this, like this, this, this," His voice begins to echo in my head.

What's happening? Why is there an echo reverberating so loud in the kitchen?

"We can't, can't, can't, can't." More echoes.

Jonah's face starts to blur. Out of fear that I might lose this moment, I close my eyes and press my lips against his, not caring about his bruises or his hurt lip. His kisses are soft like satin and so incredibly good.

When I open my eyes again, JJ is gone and I'm drooling on one of Gram's satin-cased pillows. What just happened? Was none of that real? I close my eyes again as if I can go back to wherever I was, but I can't. The only good news is that my headache is gone. I look in my bag for my phone. There are a bunch of texts from Jessa.

Jessa: *Call me. JJ got in a fight with Trevor!!!*

Whoa. Wait, what? How did I dream he'd been in a fight?

I call Jessa. "Gurl," she says when I answer. "I can't believe you fought three girls. I heard you whooped one of em with a wig. Is that true?"

"Sort of. What happened with JJ and Trevor?"

"Well, there's rumors going around that you let Trevor see your goods and he's being very crass with the details."

I wait for Jessa to say more but when she doesn't I press her.

"*And?*"

"*And* isn't it obvious? JJ went to war for you. Heard he messed Trevor up real good. I didn't see it because it happened in the boys locker room. But I heard he's suspended. Wished I woulda been there cause I woulda jumped Trevor's behind."

Jessa wouldn't have busted a grape in a food fight, but I like her spunk on the matter.

She goes on and on about what she heard. As she rambles, I think about how JJ fought Trevor to defend me. Maybe my dreams are wrong. Perhaps he really does feel for me the way I feel for him.

"Jessa, I have to tell you something and I need you to promise you won't say a word."

That shuts her up. I pause for a minute, wondering if I can say the words aloud or even trust Jessa to keep this secret. Eventually, I blurt it all out. "I think…I think I might be in love with JJ."

# Twenty-Three

## Strike One

Gram isn't one to let me lay around the house just because I've been suspended. Nope. In addition to my assignments, I've deep-cleaned her whole house, dusted for cobwebs; cleaned baseboards and blinds; shelled peas and snapped green beans. Wherever Gram went, I went too. Including going to church three times for prayer meetings and crochet class. I even went to her bowling league practice and had a bunch of Senior citizens teach me how to bowl.

I'd hoped at some point, I'd be able to talk to JJ since he's suspended as well, but his mom took his phone. Plus I've been told he's been going to Memphis with his dad to help him with work.

It's finally Thursday, the night of the dance and the College tour. There's no school tomorrow, so Spring Break has officially begun. I can't go to the dance, but I'm hoping I can still go on the trip. Since Gram has a bowling league game, she takes me to Jessa's house.

"So what's your plan?" Jessa says.

"Hope and pray," I reply. "Dad has to let me go. He already paid for me. If I show up with you, he'll have to let me go."

"I hope your plan works. It'd suck to go on this trip without you. What time does the bus leave?"

"Midnight. But we need to be there by 11:15."

Jessa flops on her bed and turns on the TV. "Cool. I'm gonna binge this new show I started watching until then."

* * *

It's 11:47.

"Jess, wake up! We're late!" I yell. We'd planned to binge watch shows but looks like we fell asleep.

Jessa jumps up and scrambles around the room throwing things in her suitcase. "Dang it! I didn't mean to fall asleep."

"Me either," I mumble.

I help Jessa zip her suitcase, then we clumsily get all our things outside and into her trunk.

We get to the church parking lot at ten after midnight. Everyone is already on the bus and Dad stands there with a white Polo jacket, jeans, and a clipboard in his hands. He taps his foot impatiently while glancing at his watch.

"Sorry, Mr. Daniels," Jessa says. "We both fell asleep. It's my fault. I didn't set my alarm for the right time. It's not Clove's fault. She was asleep too and—"

My dad holds up his hand to keep her from going on. "It's alright," he says. He hands her a little care package that I helped put together weeks ago. It has mints, miniature deodorant, toothpaste, toothbrush, sanitary products for the girls and other little items.

He taps on the bus doors and it opens to let Jessa in. Dad taps on the bus again so that the driver will close the doors before I can get on.

"You're not going to let me go?" I ask.

Dad folds his arms. People from the bus windows are starting to look. The windows are tinted so I can't really tell who's who, but it's obvious that heads are turned.

"But Dad," I plead. "I told you I was defending myself and this trip is educational. We'll be viewing college campuses and you told Mama…"

My voice grows faint as I think about her but I keep going with my statement. "You told Mama that this would be good for me to figure out where I wanna go and narrow down what I wanna do."

Dad stands firm with his arms crossed. "I did tell her that, but you don't get to disrespect me the way you did. You have yet to apologize. You shouldn't ever fix your mouth to talk to me like that. Not ever."

I'm going to have to swallow my pride because I know I was wrong for what I said to him and I *really* want to go on this trip.

"I'm sorry," I finally say.

"For what?"

I try to be serious and not sarcastic or unapologetic. "I shouldn't have said what I said to you. I was wrong. But I was—"

Dad holds up a finger, "An apology with a 'but' is not an apology."

"Yes, sir."

"Look, that apology will only allow you on this trip. When we get back, you better have it worked out in your mind where you're going to stay because it's not with me."

I gape at him in disbelief.

"Don't look at me like that. If you wanna make your own rules, get fake ID's, get your nose pierced, and fight with people, then you can do it while staying at someone else's house. Not in mine."

He knocks on the bus doors so they'll open to let me on. All eyes are on me as I try to find Jessa. My mind is spinning from what he just told me. I can't believe he's seriously going to kick me out.

The bus is segregated: girls on one side, boys on the other. I sit next to Jessa. Across from her is Xavier and JJ—who's already asleep. Fortunately, he's not as bruised as he was in my dream.

Dad gets in front of the bus and goes over rules for the trip…again.

1. Boys and girls on separate sides.
2. No loud talking on cell phones.
3. Stay with your chaperone. (And no wandering off without letting them

know where you're going).

Dad gives me a steel glare when he says the last rule, causing me to sink down in my seat.

* * *

After about an hour, the bus is quiet and not as lit up with screen lights as it was before. Tired of reading, I return my book to my bag. My fingers graze the journal from Dr. O'dea. I think about writing another poem but then my phone vibrates.

**Jessa**: *Whats up with you and J?*

She texts me even though we're sitting next to each other but I suppose this really isn't something we want to discuss with the boys right across from us.

**Me**: *We haven't talked to each other.*

**Jessa**: *Y'all need to talk. I think it's sweet you think you're in love with him.*

What does she mean by *think?* I mean, I guess I don't know for sure. Maybe I'm not. That dream kind of had me shook and then with all the nice things he'd been doing for me, just seems like…I don't know. It's confusing.

**Me**: *I've always loved him. I love all of you. You're my friends.*

**Jessa**: *It's diff with you and J. I can tell.*

**Me**: *Not to change subs, but what happened with you and Trevor? Please tell me.*

I told Jessa what had happened when I went into the room with Trevor but she hadn't shared what happened between the two of them. Every time I brought it up, she said it was nothing, but I don't believe her.

**Jessa**: *Nothing*

**Me**: *I don't believe that.*

**Jessa**: *If you didn't believe it, why'd you go out with him anyway?*

Unfortunately, she has a point but I don't have an answer, at least not a good one.

**Me**: *Guess I was into him being into me or pretending that he was.*

**Jessa:** *He's definitely a pretender.*

Jessa's holding something back.

**Me**: *Jess, for real, what happened?*

**Jessa**: *Don't judge me.*

**Me**: *Never.*

I can see her fingers hovering over the keyboard as she thinks about telling me.

**Jessa**: *We hooked up a couple of years ago at band camp. I thought we had something going, but when we got back to school he acted brand new.*

Does she mean *hooked-up* as in sex? Or hooked up like they were a couple? Surely they didn't do the former, she would've told me sooner. Right? She must see a confused look on my face, so she texts again.

**Jessa**: *We had sex.*

Ohhhh. That *is* what she meant. Dang. She waited this long to tell me?

**Me**: *Why didn't you tell me? Why'd you let me talk to him?*

**Jessa**: *I told you to be careful.*

**Me**: *If you would've told me he was your first, I never would've thought twice about him.*

**Jessa**: *You have to make your own decisions and it really wasn't something I wanted to talk about. It was an awful experience.*

**Me**: *Why?*

**Jessa**: *Don't wanna talk about it anymore.*

**Me**: *Ok. I'm sorry.*

**Jessa**: *Don't be. I'm all the way over it. Not into him even a little bit but I knew that you were. My advice is wait to have sex.*

**Me**: *For how long?*

**Jessa**: *It should be with someone who loves you and you love them. Real love. Don't do what I did.*

I don't know exactly what she did, but I leave it alone. Jessa's phone goes dark. She wraps herself in her blanket and leans her head on the pillow that she has against the window.

Welp. She's done talking for tonight. I can't believe Jessa never told me about her and Trevor. I still have so many questions, but I guess they'll have to go unanswered for now.

I close my eyes and try to sleep but then my phone vibrates.

**JJ:** *You up?*

**Me:** *Nah I'm sleep.*

**JJ:** *Sorry*

**Me:** *I was kidding! How have you been? Long time no hear.*

**JJ:** *I'm sure you know by now why I got suspended.*

**Me:** *Yep. Isn't suspension fun?*

**JJ:** *Ha! Not at all. But I have to say, watching you fight 3 girls was one of the craziest things I've seen. I understand Christa but why'd you fight Tisha?*

**Me:** *Over the years she had it coming. Plus, I heard her say she was using you to get a good grade.*

It takes him a moment to text back.

**JJ:** *I know.*

He knows?

**Me:** *You know what?*

**JJ:** *Don't be mad, but we made a deal. I let her see my notes and help her pass, she had to be nice to you.*

I want to be angry but I can't. Why would he stoop to her level? Why would he even pretend to be interested in her just so she would be nice to me? I've never known anyone to do something so…so…out of the ordinary.

**JJ:** *You're mad at me aren't you?*

**Me:** *I don't know if I am or not. Why would you do that for me?*

**JJ:** *Who says I did it for you? Maybe I did it because I hated how she talked to you and about you.*

This adds another butterfly to my stomach.

**Me:** *Some people you just can't change. After spring break, Tisha will still be Tisha.*

**JJ:** *Not trying to change her. Only wanted to give you a break.*

I don't know why but that sounds like the sweetest thing ever.

**Me:** *And Trevor?*

**JJ:** *What about him?*

**Me:** *Why'd you get into a fight with him?*

**JJ:** *Not playing this game. You know exactly why. Stop acting like Jess didn't blab everything.*

She did, but she didn't. I think I know why he got in a fight, but I want him to tell me.

**Me:** *You don't even know the truth. What if what he was saying was right?*

JJ doesn't text back right away, leaving me to wonder what he's thinking. I can only imagine what Trevor must have said in the locker room. It makes me feel stupid all over again.

**JJ:** *It's not my business what you do behind closed doors I guess, but...*

**Me:** *But?*

**JJ:** *The things he said shouldn't be said about any woman/girl/lady.*

**Me:** *You didn't have to do that.*

**JJ:** *Yes, I did.*

**Me:** *Thank you.*

Gratitude seems like the best thing to say to him before I blurt my feelings prematurely. I put my phone away and take out my journal. All these feels...I gotta write them down and turn them into something poetic.

# Twenty-Four

# *Pride*

Our first school tour of the morning is Dad's alma mater, Fort Valley State University. Although our bus is an ethnic melting pot, we're still touring a Historically Black College and University, also known as an HBCU. But first, breakfast.

"Breakfast time!" My Dad announces.

Everyone piles off the bus. Some people, like Clement and JJ's brother, Zach, take time to stretch. I think they're trying to show off because they're athletes. Nevertheless, some of the chaperones decide to do the same.

We're in an area with a variety of places to eat so we can choose where we want to go.

Ah dang, I forgot my wallet.

I go back on the bus and search through the bag I packed but my wallet's not there. Maybe it's in the other bag that's underneath the bus. Most of the group is moving towards the restaurants except for Jessa who waits for me, but she's doing the pee-pee dance.

"Just go. I'll catch up," I tell her. She scurries off in the direction of the pancake house.

I search for my wallet in my overnight bag. I'm beginning to panic because it's not in there either. I check all pockets and corners, take out my clothes, shoes and everything but there's no wallet. You have got to be kidding me! How did I come so ill-prepared? I'm starving. Maybe I can ask dad for money.

He's standing outside the bus talking to the driver. Gingerly, I approach. They bring their conversation to a close as they notice me waiting.

"Yes," Dad asks, seeming annoyed. The last thing I want to do is ask him for money. Especially after he told me he's kicking me out of the house. "I, um, I can't seem to find my wallet."

Dad stares at me, no expression whatsoever. "And?"

I fidget with the zipper on my pastel blue jacket. "And so, I need some money so I can eat."

Dad folds his arms. "I'm waiting for the question. All I hear are statements."

Ugh! Forget it! He's being ridiculous and difficult. Angrily, I get back on the bus to figure this out on my own while watching my dad walk towards McDonald's. My tummy rumbles thinking about McGriddles, hot cakes and the entire breakfast menu.

**Jessa:** *R u eating?*

**Me:** *Not hungry.*

**Jessa:** *Really? Everything ok?*

**Me:** *Yep. Tired.*

I don't want to tell my friends that I forgot my money. They'll offer to pay and I don't want them to do that for me.

Whenever we travel, my Dad usually has a backpack where he leaves emergency cash in a couple of the hidden pockets. I glance back towards the windows of the bus and go to the front where his backpack is located.

I search the outside pockets before searching inside the bag. The first thing I touch is something small and smooth like a keychain. I pull it out. It's a photo keychain of him and Mama on a roller coaster at Dollywood in East Tennessee.

For a moment I forget my hunger and think about Mama. If she were here, there's no way she would let Dad treat me like this. Then again, if Mama were here, maybe I wouldn't have done the things I'd done; although I think Tisha and Christa had it coming regardless. And, I'm almost positive Mama would've been cool with me getting my nose pierced. I mean really, what had I done that was so bad?

I put the keychain back inside the bag and continue searching for money. Finally, I find $140 folded inside. I could take all of it but then he'd know it was missing. I could take just $40 and have him think maybe he'd only brought a hundred. Or I could take none of it because this is stealing.

I take $20 and zip it back up. If I stick to a dollar menu, then maybe this could last for two days. I've fasted before so I can go without breakfast as long as I can get the other meals in. Skipping one or two meals should be no problem. Oh but wait, at the end of this trip, we're going to Six Flags. I do love amusement park food.

Maybe I can get Gram to send me money. She doesn't believe in using apps, so she'll probably want to wire it. I put the $20 back inside the pouch and move away from the backpack. As I back away, I bump into someone.

"What are you doing in here?" Clement asks.

Whew! It's only Zach's friend, the guy that got his house blown away in the twister. He puts his Vols baseball cap on backward.

"Um, nothing. Just looking for something but I couldn't find it. What are you doing here?"

"I forgot my wallet," he says.

Him too? I let him by and then scroll through my phone for Gram's number. It's right in my frequent call list but I'm buying time until Clement leaves.

"Heard you got in a fight." he says.

"Yep."

"You fighting over Jonah?" he smirks.

"No. Why would you ask that? Me and Jonah are just friends. Always have been, always will be." I'm not sure if I'm trying to convince him or myself.

Clement acts like he doesn't believe me. "Sure you are." I ignore what he implies with his comment and go back to my seat. He stands in the aisle for a moment longer, as if he's waiting on me to leave.

I hold up my phone. "Gotta make a call. You need the bus to yourself or somethin'?"

"Nah," he holds up his wallet. "Got what I came for."

He walks back down the steps of the bus. I call Gram and leave her a voice message specifically telling her what I need her to do. Money transfer services are everywhere. Surely, we'll stop at a place that has one nearby.

***

Gram still hasn't called me back about the money. Skipping breakfast was hard and skipping lunch was even harder. I'd told my friends that I was sleepy and wanted to rest instead of eating. In reality, I have a headache and can't sleep because I need food.

We've toured two colleges already. Now we're at Emory University, a small, private Methodist school. I'm trying hard to pay attention but my stomach and head are speaking so loudly that it's impossible to concentrate.

It's nearly 5 p.m. and we're walking through their dining area. The food smells so good it makes my knees buckle. Xavier is walking behind me. "Yo, you alright?" he asks. "Are you fasting or something?"

I shake my head and try to keep up, walking behind Jessa. *Food. Food. Food.* That's all I can think about. *God please help me. I'm trying to be good. I don't want to steal.*

"We have a treat for you guys today," the tour guide tells us. "It's dinner time for some of us and so we want to give y'all these passes to enjoy a meal on us at our dining commons. Enjoy! And thank you for visiting our school. May God bless you!"

The tour guide hands my dad certificates and then Dad gives them to our four chaperones to help distribute. I wait for one to come to me but it never does and the chaperones have already given all their certificates away. Everyone has begun to make their way to the dining commons, leaving me and Dad standing alone.

He looks at my open palm. I feel like I've been holding it open for a long time. He's not going to give me one, I can see it in his eyes. He wants me to break down, cry, and beg. I won't do it. He's being cruel and I have yet to shed a tear. Walking away from him, I stumble and almost hit the ground but I catch myself and keep walking.

"Clove," he calls.

I refuse to turn around. Mercy, my head hurts! I need food and water…and maybe a place to lay down.

There's a bench to my left by a tree. I can see the commons in the distance and I can see my dad still standing there watching me. *No tears, Clove, you can't spare the water.* When Dad turns to go inside, I plop down on the bench, putting my head between my knees. My arms hug my legs.

I sense someone's presence in front of me but when I look up, no one's there. I put my head back down.

*"Pain will teach you, what pride won't let you learn."* Mama's voice. Hearing her makes my head snap up. In doing so, pain spreads across my forehead.

"Ah!" I wince, squeezing my eyes shut. I can see Mama's face as she repeats the same thing. *"Pain will teach you, what pride won't let you learn."*

I open my eyes. This is too trippy. I think I'm starting to hallucinate.

I think about what Mama's voice said. Maybe I am being too prideful. I'm in pain but I won't ask for help nor will I go to my dad. The problem I'm faced with now is that I'm too weak to walk back to the dining commons.

This time I rest my elbows on my knees and let my hands massage my forehead to try and alleviate some of the pain. The presence I sensed before comes back to me, but this time it smells like soap.

Keeping my head down, I open my eyes. The shoes I see look like JJ's.

"Clove, come with me," JJ says, extending his hand. The sunlight bouncing off of his hair gives him an angelic appearance, it's as if he's glowing. I must be hallucinating.

My hand reaches out but I'm not sure I'm going to touch anything. This doesn't seem real. JJ's grip is firm, taking my hand in his and pulling me to my feet. His arm comes around my waist, holding me firmly against his side.

Not wanting him to know I'm weak, I try very hard not to lean into him but my knees buckle once again. JJ's hold is strong, keeping me steady so that I won't fall.

His low voice speaks over my head. "When's the last time you ate?"

I'm trying to remember but can't. My knees wobble so I grip his waist. His hand covers mine, holding it firmly in place.

"Hold on to me," he says.

I had no plans of letting him go.

He walks me inside and over to my dad. I have a choice to make and JJ can't do it for me.

"Pride..." the voice repeats in my head. "Pain..."

People from our group see me walk in, clinging to JJ. I feel like all eyes are on me. I turn my head into JJ's arm, my pride not letting me say what I need to say. Plus, it's twice as embarrassing with people watching.

"Clove," JJ whispers to me. "Please just ask."

I don't know how he knows what's going on. It could be that he's always observant and quite possibly has the gift of prophecy in his future.

My mind is a battlefield, warring between hunger pangs and dignity. JJ tightens his grip on my waist and it makes me stand up a little straighter.

My lip trembles and my voice is barely audible. "Dad," I begin. My dad hands me the meal ticket before I can say anything else.

# Twenty-Five

## *Strike Two*

On day two of the trip, we visit Georgia Tech, Georgia University, and Savannah College of Art and Design. I have to hand it to my dad for trying to give us a variety of programs and colleges to think about. However, I haven't seen one that I might like to attend. I have time I guess. I haven't had to skip any more meals because breakfast and lunch has been compensated by the colleges. Although I'm sure the costs were actually covered in the money we paid to reserve the tours.

Gram still hasn't gotten the money to me nor called me back. At this point, I would only need it to cover my expenses at Six Flags and anything extra I wanted to do. My relationship with Dad remains strained. We haven't said much other than a "Good morning". I suppose that's better than it was before.

Around lunch time, we stop in the AUC area where Morehouse, Spellman, Clark University and Morehouse school of medicine are located. Since neither of the schools were available for tours this weekend, my dad has given us the option to walk the campuses with a chaperone or go eat wherever we choose. Most of us are sort of over touring, and are ready to do other things. Plus many of us have already been to the AUC before, including me.

JJ, Xavier and a few other guys choose to view Morehouse, while a few girls choose to walk the Spellman campus. The rest of us pick a chaperone that's going to get food.

While people are piling off the bus, Gram finally decides to call me back so I remain on the bus to take the call privately.

"I'm sorry it took me so long to call you back, baby," Gram says. "I was helping a church member with…never mind. Now, what happened to all your money?"

I sigh and explain as I had already done in the voicemail I left earlier.

"Why doesn't your father give you some money?"

"Because he's trying to teach me a lesson. He said he's kicking me out the house when we get back."

Gram is silent for a moment. "How much money do you want me to send you?"

Finally, a little generosity from my own family.  "Can you spare two-hundred?"

"Two hundred? You do know I'm retired and on a fixed income?"

Everyone is on a fixed income. Everyone gets paid the same amount when they get their checks. Why'd she even ask how much I needed? Did she think I'd say twenty dollars would suffice?

"What can you send me then, Gram? Whatever you send I will pay you back." I had $400 saved for this trip, minus the money I spent on the nose piercing.

"I can send you one hundred. Will that work?"

I have no choice, I'll have to make it work.

"Yes ma'am," I say. "Thank you. Please text me all the details as soon as you send it."

"Will do, baby. Now you have fun and don't worry 'bout your father. I'll talk to him. Love you."

"Thanks, Gram. Love you too."

I hang up right as thudding sounds come up the steps of the bus.  It's Clement, again.

He takes his baseball cap off and scratches his head. "Why are you always on the bus?" he asks, tossing his hat to his seat like a frisbee.

"I could ask you the same," I say.

He goes to his seat. Something is suspect about Clement. Why is he always getting back on the bus?

****

Jessa and I decide to go to the Underground mall and wait for JJ and Xavier to finish their walk-through of Morehouse. After they finish, we head to a restaurant to grab a late lunch. Once they're done, we go to a restaurant to have a late lunch. We're just finishing up when my dad sends me a text.

**Dad:** *Where's my money?*

**Me:** *What money?*

He calls me in lieu of texting. "Don't play dumb with me, Clove. I had a hundred and forty dollars in my backpack's secret pocket. The secret pocket that only you knew about. And it's gone."

"And you think I stole it?"

My reaction and words get the attention of my friends. Their faces show looks of concern. So that they won't hear the rest of my conversation, I get up from the table and walk out of the restaurant.

When I find a spot where I can talk semi-privately, I say, "I didn't take it. Why would I?"

"Oh you have plenty of reasons to have taken it. I can't trust you anymore, Clove."

I put my hand to my chest. Stunned by his accusation, my voice won't come out at first. "I didn't take it. I swear! My friends paid for my lunch today and I called Gram to wire me money."

"Your Gram doesn't have the money you had saved. She's not going to send all of that."

"I know, she's only sending me one hundred."

Dad half laughs and I can tell he doesn't believe me. In his mind, I'm a thief and untrustworthy. "Well, Buttercup...no actually, you're not my little Buttercup anymore. Don't know what happened to that little girl," he mumbles.

I want to tell him I'm right here. I'm not little anymore, but I'm still his daughter. I've done nothing to him for him to treat me this way. I've been a good girl my whole life. I've gone to church, well except for these past few weeks, but even Mama Jourdan said it was hard for her to return to church after *her* mom passed. But I've been good. I didn't sneak out when I could have and I've never missed curfew. Why is he doing this to me?

"You owe me that hundred when you get it."

My anger returns. "You can't be serious. I didn't steal it! Why don't you believe me? If you take the hundred Gram gives me then that leaves me with nothing. This is bull crap!"

I don't say *crap* though, I use the other word.

"When and where did you get such a potty mouth and feel like you can talk to me with it? This is what I'm talking about. You're disrespectful and until you learn some respect you can't live with me anymore."

He hangs up on me. Anger and frustration course through me. "Ugh!" I scream.

I start walking, without a clue where I'm going. My friends are all texting and calling me, but I don't want to talk. So I keep walking.

After about twenty minutes or so, I find myself in Centennial Olympic Park. I sit down in the cool grass and watch kids play. I see couples walking, people running, jogging and walking their dogs. It's such a pretty day, too pretty to be going through all of this drama. Sometimes, I wish I still lived here and that I'd never left when I was a kid.

A thought hits me. I was born in Atlanta. Lived here for the first eight years of my life. Mama's sister, Aunt Didi, lives here. I search through my phone and silently pray she'll come get me.

Aunt Didi answers. "Hey niecy niece! What's up?"

"Aunt Didi, I'm in Atlanta. Do you think you can pick me up?"

"*Where* in Atlanta?" she asks.

I push my location button on my phone and wait a few seconds for it to go through.

"Clove, dear, you're pretty far from where I live. It might take me about an hour to get to you. Where is your father? Are you here by yourself? How'd you get here?"

"I'm on a college tour, but my dad is being stupid and…and I ran away sort of."

I didn't quite run away, but that's what I'm thinking of doing. Forget this tour! I don't have to go back with my dad if I don't want to. He's already told me he's kicking me out.

"My dad is kicking me out of the house," I say.

"He's doing what?! Oh my gawd! Stay where you at. Matter of fact, turn on your location app, so I can find you. I'll be there as soon as I can."

I turn on my Find My Friends app and invite Aunt Didi to use it to track me. I don't use the app often, but today it comes in handy. As soon as I turn on my location, JJ, Xavier and Jessa are alerted to where I am.

**Jessa:** *We're coming to the park. Stay there.*

While I wait for my friends, I take my furry blue journal out of my backpack, grateful that I'd brought it with me and not left it on the bus.

I turn to a fresh clean sheet and try to put my anger and emotions into words. But I can't. I don't feel like writing, so I let my mind wander to other things. Like how tomorrow we're supposed to be going to Six Flags before we head back to Smalltown and I promised JJ that I'd ride Goliath with him. Even earlier today, we discussed going to the aquarium together. I'd been to the aquarium when I was little, but I wanted to go again, specifically with JJ because I knew his eyes would light up seeing all the animals. He would also probably give more information than the info cards on the wall.

Once I see my friends in the distance, I breathe a sigh of relief. They join me in the grass.

Jessa sits to my left and pulls me into a hug, while JJ sits to my right and Xavier across from me. "So your dad thinks you stole something? Is that what's going on?" Jessa asks, releasing me.

I nod, knowing she probably gathered that much from my conversation at the table.

"What does he think you stole?" Xavier asks.

"His money." I give them a brief play by play of what happened, including me taking the money but putting it back. By the time I finish talking, all of them are in complete silence. I can't tell if they think I'm innocent of the alleged crime so I clue them in. "I didn't take it," I say. "I put it back."

"We know, we believe you," Jessa says. "But why doesn't your father believe you? He's being a jerk."

I agree with Jessa. "Exactly, that's why I called my Aunt Didi. She's picking me up."

Jessa's eyes widen. "Wait, what? You're leavin'? For how long?"

I shrug. "I don't know. Until my dad stops being a jerk."

"I feel responsible for some of this," Xavier says. "I never should've given you that fake I.D."

Jessa looks at him incredulously. "This has nothing to do with you, Xave. Like, at all. Mr. Daniels is wrong. How is he gonna be a youth pastor and then kick his own daughter out of the house? See, this is exactly why I stopped going to church. Too many hypocrites."

I roll my eyes. Here she goes with another rant on hypocrites in the church.

"Jess, hypocrites are everywhere, church is no exception," JJ says. "There will always be a good and bad side to everything. You make a choice to focus on one over the other."

Jessa bites her nails. He's right and she knows it. Shoot, I know it too.

Jessa spits one of her nails out to the side. "I wonder who really took the money."

"I suspect Zach's friend, Clement," I say. "He is always on the bus whenever no one else is."

Jessa thinks. "Hmm. Well, his family did lose everything in the tornado. But shoot, I'll say I did it and give you a hundred dollars so you can stay on the trip with us."

I shake my head. "No, I want my dad to believe me and stop being so cruel. He thinks I'm a liar and a thief. As far as I'm concerned the only thing I've really done wrong is get my nose pierced with a fake I.D."

Xavier groans. "See, it *is* my fault."

"No, it's not," I reassure him. "I asked for the I.D. but I didn't have to use it. I made the choice. Just like I'm making the choice to leave this tour and go with my Aunt Didi."

Jessa seems frustrated and shakes her head. "This isn't right. You can't leave. You and JJ are the whole reason me and Xavier came on this tour. I already knew where I was going to school, so I only came to spend time with y'all. I don't want you to go."

"I don't want to," I say. "But my dad is being really unfair and I think staying with my Aunt Didi is my best option right now."

My friends get quiet again. Perhaps they think I should stay and work things out with my dad, but I don't know how. I can't make someone believe me.

"I really like Morehouse," Xavier says, changing the subject. "I know I'm late, but I'm thinking of applying."

"Aw Xave, you found one you like?" I ask jubilantly.

JJ shakes his head. "Nah, he found some girls he likes. He's got, like, five numbers already."

"Stop snitchin'," Xavier says with a laugh. "Should I tell them how many girls tried to put their number in your phone?"

JJ grins a modest grin, and for the first time, I realize his braces are off. His teeth are so straight and pretty. Braces are a gift from God.

"Isn't Morehouse an all boys school?" Jessa asks. "Where'd y'all meet girls?"

Xavier briefly explains that there were some girls around but JJ was exaggerating on the numbers. I look back and forth between Xavier and JJ. You couldn't have told me that when I met them, they'd become buff, outspoken, and the type of guys girls go crazy for.

"You guys are becoming such stud muffins," I say, jokingly.

"Stud muffins?" JJ frowns. "I've never heard that before in my life."

"I think she borrowed that term from her Gram or something," Xavier teases.

"Does your Gram say things like, the cat's pajamas?" Jessa asks.

JJ's face is full of confusion. "Cat's pajamas? What does that mean? Clove, does your Gram have a cat?"

Jessa busts out laughing and tries to explain. "It is an old term, but a long time ago, if someone was the *cat's pajamas* it meant they were pretty cool."

JJ nods. "Oh. Okay. It still doesn't make sense to me. But I guess seeing a cat in pajamas would be pretty cool."

Picturing a cat in pajamas, I start to laugh. "What if it was a cat wearing cat pajamas?"

JJ starts laughing too. "That'd be hilarious."

Jessa, thinking we're being silly rolls her eyes. "You two are goofballs… perfect for each other." She said the last part under her breath, but I heard her. I'm hoping JJ didn't. I swear she better not give my secret away.

"Speaking of cats," JJ says, taking out his phone. "Did you guys know Clove sang Karaoke at a bar once?"

Two questions pop-up in my mind. One, what did he mean by *speaking of cats*? Two, how does he know about my Karaoke?

Jessa looks at me with surprised eyes. "You sang? When? You hate karaoke."

"How do you know about that?" I ask JJ "And why did us talking about cats make you think of me and karaoke?"

JJ smiles, but doesn't answer me as he taps on his phone and tosses it to Xavier. Jessa scoots in close to watch. Soon my voice belts out the tunes of Whitney Houston's *I Wanna Dance with Somebody* from the night I went out with Mama Jourdan and her friends. Hearing myself, I can see why our cat conversation led him to thoughts of my singing. I sound absolutely horrible, like a cat in distress. I cover my face. I'm not mad, just really embarrassed.

"Oh my god, I can't believe your mom recorded me and shared it with you."

"She didn't share it with me to embarrass you," JJ says. "She showed me so I can see how brave, carefree, and confident you were—are. When I saw you singing on stage, I thought, there's that girl I met in 3rd grade. Confident, carefree, brave and sassy Clove Daniels out there exploring her facets."

I smile to myself, soaking up the compliments he's giving me. Even though at first, he compared me to a cat. He wasn't wrong though. "Singing isn't one of my facets," I say.

He shakes his head. "Definitely not, but at least you tried."

We both chuckle at that fact.

"You know what other *facets* I've explored?" I say.

"What?"

"Poetry and running with you at the crack of dawn."

He grins slightly and I'm captivated by his smile. "I really enjoy running with you in the mornings. I'd love to hear some of your poetry when you're ready to share."

*Love.* He said the word. My heart is racing a mile a minute. I think about the dream I had the other night and know I'm blushing. I think I'm ready to share my poetry. In fact, I think I have a poem in my head right now. It'll go something like love, love, love, love, love, love, love.

"Here you go, J," Xavier says, tossing JJ's phone back to him. It breaks me and JJ's gaze. The gaze I didn't even realize was happening until now.

"You got a text," Xavier says to him.

JJ checks his phone. I'm close enough to see that the text is from Hannah. *I got an extra ticket to the Aquarium. You wanna come with?*

JJ doesn't respond. Instead he puts his phone back in his pocket.

"Me and Jess were going to go to the Coca Cola Museum," Xavier tells us. "If your Aunt is going to be awhile, Clove, why don't you and J come with us?"

I'm still thinking about the message JJ got from Hannah. I know she likes him, but does he like her? Are they seeing each other? Why didn't he respond? Plus, I thought he and I were going to the aquarium today. Then again, I can't leave with my Aunt and go with him. Aunt Didi said she'd be here in about an hour. That's not enough time to go through the aquarium.

"Actually," Jessa says, carefully eyeing me and JJ. "Maybe you two should stay here and…you know…." she motions with her hands. "Talk."

She smiles a knowing smile and I'm slowly regretting telling her what I told her. "I'm good with staying here," JJ says, leaning back on his elbows. He looks at me. "You okay with that? I can wait with you until your Aunt gets here."

I nod. "Yeah. Thanks. I guess we'll stay here while yall go to the Coke factory."

Jessa chuckles. "You make it seem like we're going to do drugs. But yeah um, you two have fun. Text me later and let me know details about whether you're staying with your aunt or not."

Xavier gives me a two finger salute from the forehead, nods to JJ and begins to walk away. Jessa walks backwards and mouths to me, *Tell him.*

## Twenty-Six

# *I'm Out*

Once Xavier and Jessa are gone, JJ takes off his jacket and lays down in the grass, resting his hands underneath his head. He seems relaxed, which is great, but I have questions. Particularly about the text from Hannah.

*Don't ask, Clove. It's none of your business. You don't have to know everything. Be cool, chill.* "Are you going to meet Hannah at the aquarium?" So much for being chill.

His expression doesn't change even though I've made it obvious that I saw the text.

"No," he says.

"But I thought you really wanted to go. You've never been."

"I haven't been to the Atlanta one, but I've been to the one in Chattanooga. It's not a big deal. I don't have to go."

"Oh," I say, wondering if he's only saying that because he wants to stay here with me. "Don't you think you should tell Hannah if you're not going to meet her?"

He takes his phone out of his pocket, unlocks it and texts the words *Thanks, but not this time.* He tucks his phone back in his pocket.

Satisfied for the moment, I open my blue, furry journal and search for a pen so I can write. I mean to let this whole Hannah thing go, but I can't. I have more questions.

"Have you gone out with Hannah before?"

For a second I swear I see a small smile on his face. "We've hung out before."

"Hung out like a date?"

"No, not like a date, just hanging out."

"What's the difference? Hanging out and dating?"

JJ twists his lips to the side, thinking. "This is just my take on it, and you can tell me if I'm wrong, but I think a date is when you set an appointed time and place to meet with someone. Hanging out is when you happen to be at the same place at the same time and end up enjoying each other's company."

That's a good way of defining it.

He nods towards my journal. "Is that your book of poetry?"

"Yes. Where all did you and Hannah enjoy each other's company?"

JJ sort of laughs. "You're not going to let this go, are you?"

Should I? We used to tell each other everything, but somehow and at some point in time, something changed.

I shake my head no and he lets out a small sigh. "Hannah goes to our church, right? We've had small group meetings at her house before. There have been times in the past that my parents have been a little late picking me up afterwards, so Hannah and I would talk until they arrived. Another time, I was at the library and she was there too. So we sort of sat down in one of the aisles and talked about a book she was reading. Skating rink, at your birthday party. We hung out a little, since I wasn't really all that great at skating. See, not dates, just happenstance."

Yeah well it seems to me their happenstance is happening a little too much. She's interested in him. But if I ask any more questions it'll seem like I'm jealous. Wait, am I jealous? Instead of dwelling on it, I switch topics. "Wanna hear something I wrote?"

"Of course I do," he answers. He stares at the sky as I read him the poem I wrote the first time we watched the sunrise. It's the same one I read for Dr. O'dea.

After I'm done, JJ blinks astonishingly. "Wow, that's really good. I told you

you're a good writer."

"Thanks," I say meekly.

"Anything else?"

I lay back against my backpack and open the page to something I wrote last night.

*If love is forever take me to your infinity*
*Caress my soul, bring me sweet serenity*
*Stars are like connecting dots, a roadmap of your face*
*They pull me into your love, into your open space*
*Your love is like an abyss*
*A galaxy of emotions that engulf me into bliss*

*My heart cries out for you but my mind undecided*
*Asteroids, meteors and spaceships have collided*
*Into my world*
*Into this girl*
*That wants to love you*
*But I don't know when to*
*Give you my heart*
*Because if you break it*
*I'll fall apart*

"I love it," he says.

"It needs a little work but—"

"No, it's perfect the way it is. Poetry is art and art is subjective. Trust me it's good. Really good."

His compliments make me feel warm all over. Our hands lie still next to each other. I inch mine a little closer to his.

"Can you read it to me again?" he asks

I read it once more. By the time I finish, the backs of our hands are touching. He begins to caress my index finger with his own, sending an electric current all through me.

"Wanna hear more?"

His eyes bore into mine. "Do you want to read more to me?"

That would mean I have to move my hand to turn the page so, no. Definitely, no. I open my palm towards the sky. It's an invitation for him to hold my hand. His fingertips meet the tops of my fingertips as if he's debating if we should do this. My heart beats faster than I ever thought possible. He's taking my breath away, drawing it in the longer we gaze. Finally, our fingers interlock and it's a connection so deep that I feel it in my head and my toes. It seems like seconds, minutes, hours, and days have passed. We say nothing. We just gaze and hold. I blink slowly and breathe deeply as my heart strings are completely in his grasp. My whole world feels different. The breeze blows gently, the sun shines brighter and the earth feels like it's stopped moving.

JJ breaks our daze and looks to the sky. "Looks like there might be a thunderstorm tonight."

I look at the sky too, it's blue and I see absolutely no clouds. "How can you tell?"

He points west, to a big, gray, bushy, cloud. "That big cloud over there is a thunderhead. See the way it projects out of a cumulus cloud."

I love his brain. "Tell me more."

He talks more about the clouds and lightning, then breaks down how sound travels. I've heard this all before, but I like hearing it even more right now.

My cheeks hurt and I think it's because I'm smiling so much, watching him point up to the sky and talk as though he's not a shy boy. Our hands are still locked together and mine is sweating but I don't know if he notices or just doesn't care.

I feel something warm on my ankle. Warm and wet. What is that? I bolt up and see a small dog with its leg hovering my ankle as though I'm a fire hydrant or tree. I shake my leg and scream for the dog to go away.

A lady runs over. "I am so sorry. He got off of his leash and I just couldn't get him in time. Really sorry about that," she says.

"Oh my gosh! My shoes! My pants! I can't walk around with dog pee pee ankle!"

I'm seriously upset about this but from the corner of my eye, I can see JJ has his hand over his mouth, trying not to laugh.

The lady digs through her purse and gives me a fifty dollar bill. "This is all the cash I have on me. I hope that can help pay for something for you. Once again, I really am sorry."

She runs after her dog. "Chase!" She calls after him. Well, the darn dog certainly has the right name.

JJ's lips are tucked in and I can see the corners of a smile unsuccessfully being suppressed.

"Go ahead and laugh," I tell him. He falls back in the grass and laughs hysterically. I might find it funny if my ankle weren't so cold right now.

"Clove, I am so sorry, but when you said 'dog pee pee ankle,' that was the funniest thing I've ever heard." He cracks up laughing again, and this time I have to laugh because he has one of those laughs that's so funny that you can't help but laugh too.

"What are y'all laughing about over here?"

That's Jessa's voice.

Xavier is right behind her. "Coke museum is really crowded. We're going to go back a little later."

"Seriously though, what's so funny?" Jessa asks. "I haven't seen JJ laugh this hard since the day you fell in that pot hole after school."

JJ starts cracking up all over again. I click my tongue. It wasn't a pothole. I was running after them across the school yard. There was some type of hole that must have been dug by an animal or something, but I sunk into it, buckling at the knees and then face planting into the grass. As soon as I told them I was okay, both Xavier and JJ laughed until it brought tears to their eyes. Very similar to what seems to be happening to JJ now. He wipes at his face, sits up, and tries to explain what happened.

"This dog came over and pee'd on Clove and…she has….she has… dog…" He can't even finish his sentence.

"A dog peed on my ankle," I finish for him.

Xavier puts his hand over his mouth, I can tell he's already laughing.

"Oh no! Now you have dog pee pee ankle!" Jessa says, trying not to laugh too.

JJ falls back down into the grass clutching his stomach and Xavier busts out laughing while slapping his knees. I swear he's the only person I know under the age of 64 who slaps his knees.

"I'm so happy to amuse y'all."

My pants leg feels awful. Cold, wet and stinky. Great. The good thing is that I got fifty dollars out of it. I get up and shake my leg free from the grass that tries to stick to it. "My aunt should be here by now," I mumble.

That squelches everyone's laughter as they start to remember that I'm leaving the college tour. Jessa reaches out to grab my arm. "Clove, wait a sec. Don't leave, please. Let us help you."

As kind as that is, I don't know how they can help. They can't change my dad's mind.

My Aunt Didi texts me: *I'm here. Parking.*

"My aunt's here," I say. "I'm probably going to go back to the hotel to grab my things and then…then I don't know. I guess, I'll see what happens after that. Maybe I'll stay with my aunt for the rest of spring break or maybe until the end of the school year if she'll let me."

"What? Whoa," Jessa says. "The rest of the school year? Seriously?"

I shrug. "My dad doesn't want me to live with him anymore. What am I supposed to do?"

"Stay with your Gram or maybe even me," Jessa says. "I'll talk to my parents."

My Aunt Didi calls.

"Hey Aunt Didi," I answer.

"Hey, can you see me on the app? If you can, walk towards me. Do you have your stuff yet?"

"No ma'am can you take me to get it? It's not far from here."

"Yeah. Come on and let's go. I've been calling your father back to back and he's not answering. I'm gonna use your phone to talk some sense into him."

I hang up with my aunt and tell my friends I have to go. Jessa is the first to hug me. "Please come back, okay? The rest of the school year won't be the same without you."

Xavier and JJ, aren't sure what to do, both of them sit in the grass seemingly lost for words.

"Well, see y'all later," I say, giving a small wave. I pivot around and take a step.

"Clove, wait," JJ says, standing to his feet. "I want whatever's best for you, but selfishly, I want to ride Goliath with you tomorrow like we talked about. That was our date. Remember?"

Butterflies fly around in my stomach. I smile, remembering the text he sent me weeks ago that sparked the conversation between us about roller coasters around the world. I agreed to ride Goliath with him. And according to his definition, it was a date.

I want to hug him and tell him that I'll be there for sure. However, I don't know if I'll see my friends tomorrow, at the end of spring break or at the end of the school year. My life feels so uncertain.

# Twenty-Seven

## Goliath

Aunt Didi talked to my dad and convinced him to let me participate in the rest of the trip, especially since my ticket to Six Flags was already paid. If there's one thing my dad detests, it's wasting money. Another thing he hates is arguing with Aunt Didi.

Last night, she called my dad from my phone and let him have it. Aunt Didi is not like my mama. When she's mad, she curses like a sailor. I think I learned some new words as she argued back and forth with him. She stuck up for me and told my dad he was wrong and that if *he* doesn't get it together she was going to personally kick his butt. She didn't say "butt" though. It's clear who the fighter was when she and Mama were growing up.

"You're crazy, Deidre!" my dad told her. I could hear him through the car speakers. "She ain't comin' back home 'til she remembers her manners and gives me back my money."

"Jackson, there's like what…forty kids on that bus? What makes you think it's your own daughter? My sister didn't raise no thief. My niece ain't bout that life! And then you gon' kick her out the house? What's the matter with you? Do you even know how to raise a young girl? Tell you what, Clove gon' stay down here with me. She needs you right now and you keep flying off to start a church in Las Vegas. You can't build something if all your bricks is broken. Talk to me when you figure out your life!"

"Fine. Keep her. I'll send her things."

Those words have hurt like fire. He doesn't want me, made me feel as if I was a burden. Somehow when I lost mama, I lost both my parents and it hurts so bad. I still can't figure out what I could've done to make him hate me so much.

I hadn't gotten much sleep last night, but I was determined to be on Goliath with JJ and see my friends one more time. I texted them last night to tell them I'd be at Six Flags, but I hadn't told them about my potential move-in with my Aunt.

Aunt Didi drops me off at the entrance and I spot our group right away. Jessa waves me over, giving me a big hug when I arrive. My dad is in the middle of a lecture on kindness, manners and being respectful— a lecture that I feel he needs to listen to himself.

He hands everyone a ticket and tells each person to have a good time. Except for me. I'm the very last to get my ticket and he won't even look at me when he hands it to me. That definitely stings but I shrug it off and pretend as if it doesn't hurt.

Jessa uses a scrunchie to pull her hair into a messy bun while JJ and Xavier look at the map trying to find which roller coaster we should start with.

JJ pushes his glasses up on his nose. "I say we start small and then go big because Clove's never been on a roller coaster before," he tells Xavier.

"No, we should start big and do all the upside down ones first so that we don't throw up after we eat later," Xavier counters.

"Let's start with *Goliath*," I suggest. "Go big or go home right?"

"Are you sure?" JJ asks.

I nod. "Yep! Let's go!"

I start walking but then I don't know which way to go so I turn back around and walk next to JJ. He navigates us to where it's located. Jonah was right about the weather. A large storm came in last night, so the pavement is still wet. But the sun is out so things should dry up and warm up soon.

I shudder a bit. Mostly from the rain-cooled air and partially from the excitement of riding my first roller coaster. By the time we get to Goliath, there is a decent-sized line. Knowing that we'll be waiting for a while, we start talking.

Jessa asks me if I'm still making cakes and pies for Ms. Brenda. I nod and watch a coaster car speed over us.

"How much are you gonna charge her?" she asks.

I shrug. I still haven't calculated the costs of everything.

"You're baking for Easter?" Xavier asks. "If you are, my mom was talking about your mom's Seven-Up cake. You think you can make one for us? I'll pay you."

"Sure, but you don't have to pay me, Xave." I'm not 100 percent sure I can make Mama's Seven-Up cake. Sometimes they'd be too dry when I tried to make them by myself, but Mama had a way of making them just right.

"What are you making for Mrs. Brenda?" JJ asks.

"One Chess Pie, a Chocolate Chess, Pineapple Upside Down Cake and…" I forget the last one but quickly remember. "Oh and a Strawberry Poke Cake."

Looking at JJ's face, I can tell he doesn't know what a poke cake is. I try to explain to him the details.

He nods as though he's trying to understand. "So there's Jell-o in the cake? That's interesting. Are you going to do a trial run? I'd be interested in seeing how that tastes."

"I am. You should all come over tomorrow when I make them. I've never done the poke cake before so I'll need taste testers."

All three of my friends raise their hands to volunteer. It makes me feel pretty good until my friends start talking about their favorite things my mom used to make. I know they're only sharing their memories, but it makes me think about her and I'm starting to feel somewhat panicky. Maybe it's because I have four desserts to make—no five, if I count Xavier's cake. Or maybe it's because we're getting closer to the front of the line.

My breathing is becoming a little uneven. *Calm down, Clove. You're at a theme park. This is the kind of danger you wanted. Breathe in.....breathe out.....breathe in.*

"I loved Ms. Honey's Ginger Molasses cookies. They were so good," Jessa exclaims.

The word *loved,* echoes in my brain. *Breathe out....*

"Oh and remember when she used to give us free croissants if there were some left after school?" Xavier says.

*Breathe in....*

*Remember when* echoes. I close my eyes. I'm in front with my back away from them so they can't see me. I try to keep my focus on the roller coaster but people scream and I begin to stare at the architecture of the ride. I'd watched videos of the Goliath Coaster, but seeing it in person is different. This will be fine. It's not a big deal. I can do this. I'm just a little nervous.

*Breathe in..... Breathe out.*

"I miss her cookies."

*Breathe in....*

"I miss her pies and cakes."

*Breathe out....*

"I miss all of it," Jessa says.

When the line moves again, JJ begins giving facts about the ride. He talks about how it's the tallest and longest roller coaster ride at Six Flags over Georgia. He says it travels out of the park and over water. He starts talking about velocity, slopes, and hills.

I get the hiccups.

"Clove, you ok?" Jessa asks.

I nod, but I don't turn around. If I turn around, they'll see my face and know something's wrong. Riding Goliath first was my idea and now my friends are excited about it. The sound of a hiccup escapes my mouth, making my body jump.

"Wait a sec," Jessa says. "Clove, do you have the hiccups?"

"N-no," I hiccup. All of my friends know that I do this when I'm anxious or scared.

"Turn around then," JJ requests.

I shake my head because I don't want to. JJ steps in front of me. I don't know what he sees, but it's enough to melt his smile.

I hiccup. "D-don't look at me like that. I'm f-fine. I wanna do this."

JJ puts his hands on my shoulders. "But you don't have to. We can get out of line right now." "No, we're going," I command. "I w-want to."

The line moves so I sidestep JJ and get back in front. If I've counted correctly, after the next group, it'll be our turn.

"We can sit in the back," Jessa says.

"No, that's worse. We should sit in the middle," Xavier argues.

"We're going to be in front." I tell them. I meant what I said: go big or go home.

JJ mumbles something about me being stubborn but I close my eyes and focus on breathing. This is silly. It's only a roller coaster. *Chill, Clove.*

I'm trying to be chill but my mind goes back to what JJ said about Goliath being seventy miles per hour. But I end up thinking about how seventy miles per hour was how fast the drunk driver was going.

I hiccup even more; bouncing my leg and shaking my hip. To take my mind off of things, I pivot around to face my friends. "Do y'all realize this goes seventy miles per hour? That's how fast that chick was going when she hit my mama. Crazy right! Insane. Who drives that fast in Smalltown? Full of alcohol driving seventy miles per hour on a busy street. Did you know that every fifty-two minutes a person is killed by a drunk driver? And..." My mouth spews facts of information about drunk driving like an erupting volcano.

I notice my friends watching me with wide eyes, but I can't stop talking.

The next coaster train pulls up. As soon as the previous riders exit, I go straight to the front. JJ sits in the car with me while Xavier and Jessa take the car behind us. My leg is still bouncing.

"Clove," JJ says. "We really don't have to do this."

I hear him, but I'm afraid if I open my mouth I'll throw up. Maybe he's right. I shouldn't do this.

"Do you hear me?" JJ says. "It's not too late."

I turn around. Everyone has boarded and is being fastened into safety harnesses. *I can do this, I can do this, I can do this.*

"I know you can," JJ says. "But now doesn't have to be the time."

I didn't realize I'd said those thoughts aloud. But I must have. How else would he know I said it?

I close my eyes, hiccup, and try to breathe as the car begins to move towards the incline. I make the mistake of glancing down. The ground gets farther away.

"Don't look down," JJ says.

I look down anyway. My eyes watch the crowd while my brain calculates how bad it might hurt if we plummet to the ground.

"Clove, look at me," JJ has to yell over the loud clicks that take us up.

This time, I don't want to look into his eyes because for the first time since Mama died, my tear ducts have decided to start working. We're practically perpendicular to the sky now, directly facing the clouds. My tears fall back to my ears.

JJ takes my hand and holds it tight. "It's going to be alright. This ride is like life; up and down, scary and fun, good and bad times. But I promise you, it's going to be okay. Scream, cry, do whatever you want…I'm right here."

I'm so grateful that he is. I squeeze his hand and scream right before the ride drops.

# Twenty-Eight

# Forgiveness

Once the ride is over, I run ahead of my friends. My eyes are filled with tears, blurring my vision. Roller coasters are supposed to be thrill rides but I wasn't thrilled. Instead, I feel like I went through yet another traumatic experience. Unashamedly, I admit to myself that I want my dad.

I reach into the small bag Aunt Didi bought me and take out my phone to call him but then I remember that he hates me. If I call he probably won't answer.

Jessa calls me but I don't answer. Xavier calls and then JJ but I don't answer any of them. I find a restaurant and sit in a back booth near a window. Not many people are inside, which is fine for me.

"You alright?" a waiter asks me.

I nod while wiping away my tears. "Could I have a ginger ale, please? Do you have that?"

"Yep. We do now because so many people feel queasy after the rides. I'll bring you that and some soda crackers."

I put my head down on the table and continue letting the tears fall. The waitress puts the soda down along with a plate of crackers. When I look up to thank her, my dad is sitting across from me. How did he find me?

He shows me his phone. "Locator."

Oh yeah. I forgot he has access to it. He's known where I've been this whole time.

"Why are you here?" I sniff.

"Why wouldn't I be?" he asks.

I find this to be an incredulous question. "Because you hate me. Because you've accused me of stealing from you. Because I cursed you; disappointed you and because you think it's my fault mama's gone. "

I hadn't realized it until the words came out of my mouth, but dad probably really does blame me for mom's death. After all, I was the one who forgot my skates. If she hadn't gone back to get them, none of this would've ever happened.

Several seconds pass, maybe even a minute or two, and Dad doesn't respond, just looks down at the table. Finally, he clasps his hands together on the table and says, "You're right. I blamed you."

My heart drops lower than I thought it could ever go. Although I'd said the words, it hurts worse to hear him say it.

His eyes fill with tears. "As a parent, I felt like I wasn't supposed to blame you, I was supposed to tell you it wasn't your fault. I was supposed to be the one to tell you that things happen and God's plan is perfect, but I couldn't even believe those things myself. So you're right. I've blamed you and I've been angry with you."

Covering my face, I cry uncontrollably into my hands, feeling worthless and unloved. But then I feel dad slide into the booth next to me. His arms comfort me. "Forgive me," he says. "I haven't been a good father to you these past few months."

I can't stop crying and therefore, I can't speak either.

Dad squeezes my shoulders. "Do you know who paid me a visit yesterday?"

I don't answer.

"Your mom."

Instantly I stop crying and look at him like he's crazy.

With a tear falling down his cheek, he smiles. "I'm not crazy. She came to me in a dream and scolded me for the way I've been treating you. She sounded alot like your Aunt Didi. Can you believe it? Your mother coming from the grave to go off on me?"

That makes me laugh and dad laughs too.

"What did she say?" I ask.

"She told me she loves me, she loves you and she's not angry with anyone. She told me that as long as I'm angry with you and angry with the drunk driver, I'm going to become a bitter old man who lives alone."

I try to envision mama talking to dad in a dream; what she might have looked like, what she was wearing, or how she sounded. I wish mom could have visited me as well.

"It's not your fault," Dad says. "The person that was drunk driving was in a dark place, and that darkness inside of her caused her to take away someone who was really special to a lot of people."

Taking several napkins from the dispenser on the table, I blow my nose.

"Your mom was my best friend," Dad says. "We'd been friends since we met at Youth Camp when she was seventeen. She wrote me letters. I know you think we're super old because we wrote letters, but she liked the idea of putting pen to paper. It meant more to her than sending an email. She would write to me every week and she kept on writing even after we got married."

I know he knew my mama longer, so I can't imagine how he must feel losing someone he'd known for so long. Truthfully, I hadn't really thought about it until now.

Dad continues, "And you know, JJ's mom has been suffering too. Your mother was her best friend. Shortly after moving back here, she lost both of her parents and now she's lost a best friend. JJ's mom may seem strong, but James has said she's cried every morning."

I didn't know that she was hurting as well but it makes sense. I can't imagine losing any of my best friends.

"Your Aunt Didi lost a sister. Your uncle lost a sister-in-law. People at the church lost someone they would confide in and people at the bakery lost a really good baker. You know how your Mama got the name Honey?"

I do know, but Dad proceeds to tell me anyway.

"She always did kind things for people. Even when she was hurting, she was a light. She'd bake something when she was off work and take it over to people who were hurting too. Honey would stay up late or get up early and say, 'I have to bake this cake for so-in-so, she just lost her dog,' or she'd say, 'Sista Brenda is upset about her son going overseas, I'm going to bring her this dessert.' She always said something sweet makes the heart feel better."

Tears fall down my face relentlessly.

"Believe it or not," Dad says. " I think your Mama has passed her heart of service and baking talents to you."

I do love baking and I've kinda been looking forward to making desserts for Ms. Brenda but I'm also nervous. What if I mess up? Or it doesn't turn out right? Mama won't be here to help me.

"Giants," Dad says. "Big things in life that come our way when we don't expect them. Your Mama's death was a giant. It knocked me down, but not out. This week has been a reality check for me. I was wrong to kick you out, to accuse you of stealing and to make you feel like I didn't want you. Last night, in that dream, I got a dose of reality."

"Nah, you got the wrath of Mama."

Dad laughs. "True. I wasn't expecting that. But something else your mother said was if I'm hurting, I have to remember that the best way to heal is to be of service to others. She's right. So I'm starting with you right now by apologizing for my actions and asking for your forgiveness. I'm sorry that I haven't been very understanding or available. After your mom passed, I got tunnel vision and started focusing on something else to take my mind off my hurt. Starting a church in Las Vegas isn't nearly as important as being here for you."

I hug him. "I forgive you, dad. I'm sorry for getting a fake I.D. and for running away."

That's all I apologize for, because everything else I did feels justified in my mind.

"Also, I know you didn't steal the money," Dad says.

I'm glad he finally believes me. I'd obviously tried to starve myself before taking his money.

"How do you know?" I ask.

"For one, you have too much pride, which may or may not be a bad thing.

Two, another student confessed to taking the money. Three, I found three one hundred dollar bills in my bag last night. I think it's safe to say your friends really love you."

There's no doubt JJ, Jessa and Xavier tried to clear my name on my behalf. Dad nods towards the window where all of them are standing outside, trying not to be nosy but failing miserably. I may have lost one of the closest people in my life, but one thing is for sure: I have some pretty awesome friends.

## Twenty-Nine

# F.R.I.E.N.D.S.

My apron is covered in flour. I've been in the kitchen since we got back from our trip. We got in around six in the morning and I'd sent my Dad straight to the store with a list of ingredients I needed.

I wanted to do a trial run on the Strawberry Poke cake because I've never made it before. My friends are coming over at four o'clock to taste test so I've got about four hours until they get here. I wipe my forehead with the back of my hand trying to push back a loose strand of hair that's wiggled its way out my low bun.

The kitchen is a mess. Instead of making only one cake, I decided to do a few extra things. What dad said about doing something nice for someone else really stuck with me. So I decided to do something nice for Clement and his family. Zach told me that Clement liked my Mama's Strawberry Rhubarb pie and luckily Dad was able to find rhubarb.

On the bus ride back, while everyone was asleep, I researched more information about Mama's accident. Trevor had been right about the drunk driver having kids. She had a little girl and a baby. I want to meet them so I'm baking something for them as well. Their mother was to blame for the accident, but they had done nothing wrong.

Dad thinks I'm taking on too much but I really want to do something nice for people and this is the only way I know how. I continue rolling dough, chopping rhubarb, slicing strawberries, and building the perfect lattice crust to go on top. I'm also making a Pineapple Upside Down' cake so I've got the pineapple slices soaking in a brown sugar syrup. The strawberry cake just needs to be poked and topped with Jell-o.

I take each pineapple ring and place them one by one in the bottom of a buttered glass 9x14 dish. Next, I pour in the cake batter, scraping the sides and bottom of the bowl to make sure everything goes in.

There's a knock at the door. I know it's JJ. He wanted to see how I make the Poke cake. Wiping my hands on my apron, I quickly open the door, then run back into the kitchen.

The oven beeps letting me know that it's preheated and ready for the pie. Carefully, I place the pie inside and close the oven door.

JJ scans the kitchen with his eyes wide in disbelief. I know it's a mess but I'll clean up later.

"What can I do to help?" he asks.

Grabbing a wooden spoon, I use the handle to start poking holes in the cake. "Come see this," I tell him. JJ stands behind me and watches as I poke holes in the cake. The tea kettle on the stove starts to whistle so he reaches over to turn it off for me.

"Thanks."

"Are you making tea?" he asks.

"No, it's the hot water for the Jell-o. By the way, can you look in that grocery bag and get it out for me?"

He rustles through the grocery bags for awhile.

"Do you see it?" I ask.

"No. Could it be somewhere else?"

I search through the bags myself. Where is it? I check the receipt. It's not listed. "Oh shoot!" All of this and Dad hadn't bought the last ingredient on my list.

JJ offers to go to the store for me but, now that he's here, I don't want him to leave.

I try tossing the spoon into the sink, but fall short on my throw. It lands in the yellow cake batter, sinking down to the bottom like quick sand.

"Well, at least it was a good throw," JJ shrugs. I appreciate his optimism.

My dad walks into the kitchen and scratches his head at the disaster I've created. "What all are you making, again?"

This doesn't seem like it's going so well. Mama never made this big of a mess. "A pie, two cakes and some cookies. Dad, you forgot the Jell-o. I can't make the poke cake without it."

"Can you make strawberry syrup instead?" JJ suggests. "You have extra strawberries."

Hmmm. That's not a bad idea. I find a small pot and start tossing strawberries in it along with sugar and a little bit of water. I can definitely make strawberry syrup. My dad tells me that he has a meeting to go to but he'll be back in an hour.

"You and JJ…" Dad says cautiously. "You two will be fine 'til I get back, right?"

I glance over my shoulder and frown. "Yes, of course. We're not babies."

My dad shakes his head. "That's not what I mean. Y'all have become awfully chummy these days. When I get back the two of you better be vertical and not horizontal."

"Dad!" I know what he's trying to say and it's embarrassing. "JJ and I are just friends. You know that."

"Mmmmm hmmmm. Vertical though. Y'all better be vertical friends."

JJ's face turns the color of the strawberries "Mr. Daniels, sir, if it bothers you for me to be here while you're gone, I can leave and come back when you're here again."

My dad holds up his hand and shakes his head. "No, I trust you…just remember what I've said."

"Yes, sir," JJ says respectfully.

Once my dad leaves, JJ facepalms. "Wow," he says.

"I know, right." My dad just made it even more awkward between us. However, since he brought it up, maybe we should address it. Or at least I should address how I feel. I open my mouth to say something but nothing intelligible comes out.

"We…um…you…," I begin but I don't know how to finish.

JJ sniffs the air. "Is something burning?"

Oh no! The strawberry syrup is already burning. I stir—or more like scrape—the pot. This makes me upset. This is the third thing I've ruined.

"It's okay," JJ says getting up. "How about I go get the ingredients you need?"

A sizzling sound comes from the oven. Smoke rises through one of the stove eyes, setting off the smoke alarm.

JJ opens the windows while I check the oven. The rhubarb filling is spilling over and burning. The crust is also starting to brown way too early. I take it out and set it on top of the stove while JJ fans a pot holder over the smoke alarm.

I want to cry but now is not the time. A sad baker makes the food sad, but my tears don't seem to care. They fall without asking my permission.

Not wanting JJ to see me cry again, I turn away from him. This will be the second breakdown I've had in front of him within 24 hours. It's like a dam has broken. All the tears that I'd kept in for so long are running free.

I take the bottom of my apron and dab at my face but it doesn't help, more tears fall. When the smoke alarm finally shuts up, I can hear JJ moving things behind me, washing his hands and tearing off a paper towel.

This is such a stupid thing to get upset over. I was overly ambitious, it was way too much. "Clove," JJ says softy, tugging on my apron. "Please come here. Let me hold you."

I'm wiping at my eyes, trying to console myself but it's not working. JJ pulls me to him and I bury my head into his chest. My arms shake, my chest heaves, and my nose runs. It's an ugly cry.

"Let it out," JJ tells me. He holds me tight and rubs my back until my sobbing subsides.

"Tell me how I can help you. What should I do?" he asks.

Just this really. It seems like him holding me is all I need. I don't want him to move or go anywhere.

"Don't move." I say. He abruptly stops rubbing my back and keeps completely still.

"No silly, keep rubbing my back."

He rubs my back again.

"Hold me tighter," I say. I know I'm being somewhat demanding but I need all of this. JJ does as I say and holds me tighter.

"Your hair smells like coconuts," he says.

"Is that good or bad? Do you like coconuts?"

"I love them."

A few stray tears that didn't get the message that we're done expressing sorrow, trickle down my face. JJ lifts my chin and wipes away a tear with his thumb. Then he tenderly traces the shape of one of my vitiligo clouds with his finger.

His eyes search mine and they do that thing they do: make me feel like I'm floating on water.

Something my dad said comes to my mind. I know it's weird to think of my dad at this moment, but yesterday Dad said he and Mama were best friends before they fell in love. They'd been together for years. But now…she's gone.

I can't fall in love with JJ. I just can't. We have to be friends. Only friends.

His hand still lingers against my cheek and I cover his hand with mine. "Thank you," I whisper.

"For what?" he asks.

"For being here. For always being here. For always being my…friend." The last word that escapes me tastes like metal in my mouth. It doesn't belong.

Gradually, he drops his hand. "Anytime."

I feel like a child who's let a single scoop of ice cream fall to the ground. Is it too late to say, *just kidding, I'm in love with you?*

In one month, JJ will have this amazing opportunity to be a Counselor at two different camps. He'll be gone the entire summer. I'd also made plans to stay with Aunt Didi for most of my summer. After that, we're moving to Las Vegas. JJ and I haven't fully talked about this because I've avoided the discussion.

Moving to the sink, I wash my hands again. Then I get foil and begin covering the outer edges of the rhubarb pie.

"I'm moving to Las Vegas," I say to him.

"I heard. That's good, right? You've always wanted to get out of Smalltown."

It's good and it's bad. If it means I can't see him everyday, it's bad.

I can feel JJ watching me while I keep busy around the kitchen, ignoring my ever-growing feelings for him.

"Clove," JJ says. The way he says my name even sounds different. It gives me goosebumps and makes my heart flutter. But I don't stop moving around the kitchen. "Yes?"

"Can I ask you something?"

I draw my breath in and make light of what he just said. "Was that it? Was that the question?" I try to smile.

"No. Can you stop for a second? And that wasn't the question either. Please look at me."

I face him again, but fiddle with the apron strings behind my back and let my eyes fall to the floor.

The longer he delays, the more anxious I get. What if he tells me he loves me? Do I say it back? If this were any other time, my answer would be yes, but now I'm scared to love him, scared to lose him, and scared of what all that really means.

He takes a deep breath. "So, I'm singing at church for Easter Sunday. Do you think you could come?"

I blink repeatedly. That wasn't what I was expecting him to say, but I give him a big smile.

"JJ, that's wonderful!" Then I squint my eyes at him. "Can you even sing?" I ask jokingly.

He shrugs his shoulders while sheepishly grinning.

Easter is in less than six days. I hadn't even bought a dress or gone shopping like Mama and I used to do. We used to take a day trip down to Memphis or drive to Nashville for a girls shopping day. We'd pick a new dress and shoes, then go out for lunch and sometimes get our nails done. I haven't had a mani pedi in a long time. Thinking about Easter makes me a little sad.

"JJ, I don't know. I just ugly cried in front of you. You want me to ugly cry in front of the whole church?"

" I know. The timing is bad for you but I've been practicing for some time now and…it's just that…it makes me nervous thinking about getting up there with all those people watching me. But if you're there, I think…I mean…maybe…"

My eyes soften as his voice trails off. I know what he's trying to say. Easter Sunday is when almost everyone comes to church. For some, it'll be their first time, for others, they may be in town visiting or coming back to church after some time away. It's the most crowded service of the year.

JJ's eyes plead with me. I know he needs me for support. As much as he's been here for me, I can't say no.

"Okay," I say softly. "I'll be there."

His shoulders fall down some, relaxing at my response. "Thank you. I have just one more request."

"Yeah?"

"Can you sit in the front row?"

I grin. "Jonah Jourdan, now you're just being ridiculous."

*　*　*

I left the door unlocked so Xavier and Jessa could walk in when they got here. After all the baking and cleaning up, I should've known I'd be exhausted. What I hadn't expected was to wake up to my friends staring at me.

At first, I don't understand their gawking. But then I realize I'm not just laying down on the sofa; I'm laying down *on* JJ.

We'd heeded my father's request—sort of. We aren't *completely* horizontal. JJ is laid back against the chaise of our gray sectional with his arms wrapped around me and my head is resting on his chest. I have no idea how we got this way, but I'm so comfortable I don't want to move. This is the best sleep I've had in weeks.

I lift my head slightly and realize I've drooled on JJ's shirt. Oh my goodness!

"Dang," Xavier says. "You know you're in love when you let somebody drool on you."

Jessa snickers, then they walk into the kitchen. I should get up and be a good host, but now I feel awful that I've messed up JJ's shirt. And I'm completely flushed that my friends have seen me and JJ snuggling.

Oh well. I lay my head back down. Jessa and Xavier have been over my house too many times. They don't need me to be a host.

Pressing my ear against JJ's chest, I listen to the rhythm of his heart. My eyes close and I let my other senses take over. The warmth of JJ against me, the clean fragrance of his shirt and skin, the rhythmic sound of his heart … CLINK! CLANK! The sound of Jessa or Xavier dropping a knife.

The noise startles JJ awake so his warm hands begin slowly rubbing my back, but then stop abruptly as if he realizes what he's doing. I keep pretending like I'm sleep because I need him to hold me a little longer.

The first thing he does is clear his throat. "Um, Clove?" His voice is deep from sleep and it rumbles like thunder underneath me.

"Hmmm?"

"Xave and Jess are here."

"I know."

"Don't you think we should get up?"

I don't respond, so we stay like we are. JJ's hands smooth over my back once again. I can hear his heart beating faster. He shifts, causing me to sit up. I wipe the side of my mouth as he sees the drool spot.

"Sorry," I purse my lips together. That is super embarrassing.

JJ lifts one eyebrow along with his smile rising on one side in amusement. "Never thought I'd get a girl to drool over me."

I cover my face. "I'm so sorry, I'll get you another shirt."

I run to my room to get a tee that might fit him. Coming back, I toss a gray t-shirt at him. He catches it, opens it up, and shakes his head.

"Really? *This is my Otter shirt.* You think this will fit?"

"It should."

He goes into the bathroom to change.

In the kitchen, Xavier and Jessa have already cut gigantic slices of Pineapple Upside Down cake.

"Soooo… are y'all gonna save some cake for everybody else?" I tease .

"Gurl! You put yo' foot in this cake!" Jessa tells me.

"Yep, two feet," Xavier says with his mouth full. I chuckle. In the south, that's a big compliment. I find a saucer for JJ and prepare to cut him a slice of cake that's the same size as what Xavier and Jessa cut but then JJ walks into the kitchen wearing the shirt I gave him. It's way too small.

"My arms can't breathe," he says.

Jessa and Xavier start laughing immediately.

Well, he used to wear a medium. I cover my mouth so that I don't laugh too. He hands me something. "I got you a t-shirt at the Six Flags gift shop, but I think we may have to trade."

I unfold the shirt. It's white with a purple octopus that says: *I can slap 8 people at one time.*

I turn it around to show Jessa and Xavier. They laugh, almost uncontrollably.

"Yo, that is hilarious and so true," Xavier says.

Jessa goes on about how cute it is that JJ bought me a shirt. She also brings up something that I didn't want her to say. "So are y'all together now or what?"

I wait for JJ to say something. Are we? Does cuddling and holding hands automatically put us into a relationship?

JJ rubs a spot on the back of his neck. "Nah," he says. "Clove likes guys who talk like *dis* and do dey mouf like dis right hurr."

He mocks Trevor by curling up his lip. Next, he takes a small piece of foil from the Rhubarb pie and puts it over his tooth. "She like dem southern boi's that be like 'C'meer gul, lemme holla atchu!'"

Jessa almost chokes on her cake. "Oh my gawd JJ, that's hilarious! I had no idea you could talk like that!"

"Yeen know?" JJ continues.

Now Xavier joins in. "Sheen een know, dawg."

"Mane, sheen know! I'm bout tuh cut dis cake right hurr fah sho."

JJ's imitation of Trevor is spot on. The way JJ does his mouth, making a sneer with every word is way too cute. Okay, so he's right. I like it. Now Xavier and JJ go back and forth talking like Trevor. Jessa and I can't stop laughing.

"Kinda hard not to pick up the dialect when you've lived here for so long." JJ says. He bites into his cake slice. "Oh my goodness, Clove, you did so good on this! I told you it would be fine."

"Neither one of y'all have answered Jessa's question," Xavier reminds us.

Dang. I was hoping they'd drop the subject but I don't blame them for asking. They did walk in on us cuddled up on the sofa. If JJ and I are evolving into a relationship, will it change the dynamic of our clique? How will it work long distance?

Jessa holds the tip of her fork in her mouth. "Maybe y'all should kiss or something. Perhaps then the answer will be plain as day. What do you think, Clove?" She grins at me mischievously.

Oh my gosh. What is she doing? I knew I shouldn't have told her that I was catching feelings.

JJ looks at Jessa and then back at me. My cheeks feel so hot and all I can do is try to keep busy, but there's nothing to do. JJ washed all the dishes for me. He does kind of deserve a kiss for that.

I glance at JJ but he keeps his head down, picking at the piece of his cake. We need to change the subject to something—anything.

"What about you and Xave?" I ask Jessa. "Y'all are going to prom together. What's that mean?"

Both of the boys shift their eyes and stuff cake in their mouths almost on cue. Something's going on.

"What's up? Why y'all get quiet? Jessa can ask about me and JJ but I can't ask about her and Xave?

"Just drop it, Clove," Xavier says.

But I don't want to drop it. Now it's Jessa's turn to be put on the spot.

"Jessa, what's going on?"

She covers her face with both hands. This has to have something to do with the rumors going around school. Would I be wrong to ask? I decide to just go for it.

"Jessa, are you—

"Yes," she says, before I can finish. "The rumors are true. My parents don't know so I'm going with Xavier as a cover."

It takes too long for me to find the right words. The room is completely silent until Jessa's eyes begin to water. "I didn't know if I could tell you," she says, blinking back tears. "I thought you might…might…not want to be friends."

"Why?" I ask. "I mean, why would you think that? You're my bestie. I love you. No judgment ever."

"We all love you," Xavier says, rubbing her back.

"And we'll love whoever loves you," JJ says. The three of us gather around Jessa and giver her a group hug.

## Thirty

# *Blind Faith*

I've decided to visit the family of the drunk driver even though our lawyers advised against it. What my dad said about pushing past your pain to do something kind for others, resonated with me.

"You don't have to do this. No one is forcing you," Xavier reminds me. I'm sitting in the front seat of his car because he was the only one who could take me where I wanted to go today.

"I just wanna give them these cookies, that's all. I'm not lingering to make small talk or nothing like that," I say.

After my baking fiasco yesterday, I'd decided to wait until today to bake again.

"Have you even thought about what you're going to say? You can't exactly walk up to the little girl and say, 'Hey, your mom crashed into my mom and that's why your mom's in jail.'"

I know I can't say that. I'd thought about it as I waited for the cookies to come out of the oven but I came up with nothing.

As Xavier turns into the neighborhood, the sky changes from sunny to cloudy and back to sunny. The way I've been watching the sky the past couple months, I feel like I could dabble in Meteorology.

Xavier parks his car in front of a small, red, brick house with a handicap ramp going up the steps. There's a big tree with a tire swing attached. Toys are all over the yard, patches of grass are missing and tin pie pans surround a pile of mud. The house next to it has a broken window and the screen door is a frame without netting.

I lean my head back against the seats of Xavier's 87 Oldsmobile Cutlass. "You want me to come with you?" he asks.

Thinking, I chew on my lip. Maybe he should come with me. "No, I think I should do this by myself."

His hand touches my shoulder. "Clove, you don't have to do this alone. You don't have to do this at all."

That's the same thing my dad had said. "What you're doing is commendable," Dad told me before we left, "But I'm sorry, I'm just not ready. It's going to take me a little more time."

I understood and wasn't mad at him but I still wanted to do what was in my heart. JJ was busy doing some things with his family and Jessa just wanted to be alone today, so I called Xavier and asked if he could drive me.

I walk up the ramp to the front porch and search for a doorbell. There isn't one so I open the screen door, knock three times and wait.

I know they're in there because I hear them. Finally, a man that sort of resembles my dad opens the door. He's wearing a white A-shirt, gray sweatpants, and carrying a baby that could be around the same age as JJ's sister.

His face is unshaven and he looks like he could use some sleep. The baby boy has skin like Caleb but with curly light blonde hair and brown eyes. He sucks on a pacifier while eyeing me carefully. His green onesie pajamas are worn down on the bottom. "How can I help you?" The man asks.

"Um, I'm Clove….Daniels. I um…" I search for more words but I can't find any to say.

His eyes show recognition of my name. Another child comes to the door. She's almost identical to the baby boy but with frizzy unkempt hair around her head. Her eyes are a dull brown and seem to have a glaze over them. She holds on to the bottom of the man's shirt while staring past me.

"Hi," she waves at my stomach. "Who is it Daddy?"

The dad extends his other hand to me as if we're going to shake, but then he thinks better of it and puts his hand back down. "Almond, why don't you go play in the yard for a moment while I talk to the lady, alright?"

"Yes, Daddy," she says and lets go of his shirt. She uses her hands to guide her to the handicap ramp and uses the rail to walk down. Once she gets to the end of the ramp, she jumps as though she's made a major achievement.

"What are you doing here?" the father asks me. He sounds more curious than angry. I stumble to find the reason why; a reason that he might understand. "Well see, I…um…"

*Cookies, Clove. Give him the cookies.* I extend my arms. "My mama was a baker. She worked at the bakery downtown, *Kate Cakes and Coffee*. And so I…I baked some of her cookies from a recipe book she had and I wanted to bring them over. I was trying to um… I was trying to…but…I.."

None of my words are coming together and my eyes are starting to water. This may have been one step too big.

The guy takes the cookies. "I'm Steven," he says. "Would you like to come in?"

I shake my head and pinch the bridge of my nose, trying to keep the tears from falling. It doesn't work. Why do I keep crying in the most inconvenient moments?

"No, I'm sorry, I thought I could do this but I can't. Sorry to bother you." I turn around and almost trip down the steps.

"Wait," Steven calls after me.

My feet stop but I don't turn around.

"You don't have to say anything. Just listen," Steven says. "I can't explain why my wife did what she did because I really don't know. I feel like an apology isn't good enough. But I appreciate your heart. I'm glad you're trying to forgive."

I wipe my eyes and watch the little girl guiding her hand along the wired fence. She steps on a twig and then picks it up, using it to make noise against the fence.

"Thanks for the cookies," Steven says. "Almond liked going to the downtown bakery. Your Mama used to give her a free cookie if she could figure out where they were in the glass case. She always kept them in the same spot so Almond would know exactly where they were. Honey would give her a free cookie every time."

So they knew my mom. They'd met her and spoke with her. Mama knew this child. How ironic.

Almond tries to twirl around. She does it once, then falls. "Daddy!" she calls and looks around like she's trying to find her bearings.

"I'm over here," Steven says. "What'd I tell you about spinning? It throws you off."

My mind is trying to wrap my head around what I'm seeing. Is she blind? Almond gets up and walks with her arms extended. She finds my leg first.

"Sorry," she says.

Steven reaches out for her. "Hey sweetie, guess what? You know those cookies you like from the bakery? This lady brought us some."

Steven hands her the container of cookies and she carefully opens them. She sniffs. "Mmmmmm Ginger Molasses Cookies! My favorite!"

Her hands touch my arm and then she does something I don't expect: her little arms embrace me around the waist.

"Thank you, Miss Honey," she says. "I miss you at the shop. I thought you left. I miss your cookies. I miss your voice."

I cover my mouth to prevent myself from sobbing. My tears are unstoppable. I stoop down to hug her.

"You smell pretty," Almond says. "Remember you said you'd take me skating one day. When are we gonna go? Will I meet your daughter? Will she teach me to skate?"

I close my eyes. *God, I see you. I know what you're doing.* I take a deep breath.

"Of course," I tell her sweetly. "But guess what? I'm not Honey, I'm her daughter, Clove. Would you like to go skating with me tonight?"

She grins the brightest grin and jumps up and down. Some of the cookies fly out and fall to the ground. "Daddy, can I go? Can I go today?"

Steven looks at me sympathetically. "You don't have to do that."

"I want to. You can drive her there to meet me."

Almond is still jumping with anticipation. "Please Daddy, please!"

"Are you sure?" Steven asks me.

"I'm very sure. Six o'clock, okay? I won't keep her out late."

Steven shrugs. "Alright, then. I'll meet you there at that time. Can you take my number in case you change your mind?"

I won't change my mind but I pull out my phone anyway. After I get Steven's info, Almond hugs my legs and I pat her back.

"See you soon," I say.

She waves at me and continues waving until we drive away.

## Thirty-One

# Roll With It

JJ drives me to the skating rink. In my arms are the skates that mama gave me. I'd taken them out of the crushed up box and put them in a reusable grocery bag. I wasn't one hundred percent sure I'd ever wear the skates but if I'm teaching Almond to do this for the first time, I'll probably need to walk with her.

When Almond arrives, she can hardly keep still. "This is awesome," she shouts. "It smells like food and sort of like feet."

"That's the same thing I said," JJ mumbles.

Almond turns in the direction of his voice. "Who said that?"

JJ bends down to her level. "I'm Jonah, but you can call me JJ. And who might you be?"

"Almond. Mr. JJ, can I touch your hair? It'll help me get to know you."

"Sure." He leans his head forward and she immerses her little hands into his hair. He has it down and not pulled up today. She feels his face and touches his glasses.

"Almond, you're going to dirty up his glasses," her dad says.

Almond withdraws her hand. "Sorry. You smell good though. Like soap and sunshine."

That's it! That's exactly what he smells like. "Almond," I say. "I've been trying to figure out that scent for years and I think you've done it in less than one minute."

"Well he does. Smells just like a sunny day. Anyway, let's get some skates! I'm ready! I was born ready! Let's roll!"

*Let's roll*, Mama used to say the same thing. I take Almond's hand and guide her through the rink and over to the rentals. We get her size and her dad puts on her skates.

"Aren't you going to skate, Clove?" she asks.

"Maybe later. I'm going to help you first."

Her dad intervenes. "It may help if she can use her hands to feel how your feet move in the skates, but it's up to you."

Carefully, I pull my skates out of the bag. It's JJ's first time seeing them, so he admires them as I place them on the floor. I put my feet inside and lace up the red strings. They're a little tight, but I'm sure my feet will adjust.

"Alright Almond, sit down in front of me and I'm going to guide your hands to the top of my skates."

She sits on the ground and finds my skates by herself. "What do they look like?" she asks.

"They're white with red laces. Each wheel is a different color in the rainbow. Do you know the rainbow colors?'

"Yes. ROY G BIV. Red, Orange, Yellow, Green, Blue, Indigo, Violet. But that's only seven colors, don't you need eight wheels?"

Clever girl. I tell her that the last wheel is pink and that seems to excite her. I instruct Almond to keep her hands on top of my skates as I begin to move them in the rhythm for skating. Left then right so she can tell what she needs to do on the skate floor.

After awhile, she tells me she's ready to try it on her own.

JJ has put skates on as well. We take Almond's hands and lead her out onto the floor.

***

"Clove, I am so proud of you," JJ tells me after we leave the skating rink. "That took courage and selflessness."

"Thanks," I say, though I wasn't doing it for the accolades. For the most part, I was thinking like Dad told me. What would Mama do if she were here? How can I honor her instead of falling into a place of hopelessness? That's all I had been thinking.

We're silent so I turn on the radio. A country music song that I recognize comes on. JJ pushes a button to change the station. I change it back and he begins to smile. "The person driving has listening rights."

"You made that up," I say, pushing the button to put it back on the country song.

He changes it again. "No, I did not. Ask anyone and they will tell you the same."

I push the button again but now the song is going off. "JJ, see what you did? Now I can't listen to it."

"Why do you like that song? Do you even know what it's about?"

This makes me blush again because I don't want to tell him it's about a girl who falls for her best friend. She loves him but she's not sure if he loves her too.

I fold my arms over my chest. "If you wouldn't have kept changing the station you would've found out. Now you're sorry outta luck."

He stops at a traffic light and smirks at me. "Chloe Love Daniels. Are you being sassy with me?"

Shifting my body towards the window, I suck in my cheeks. JJ is my only friend that knows the story of how I got the name Clove. It's because my parents couldn't decide on Chloe or Love, so they mixed the two.

Once we arrive at my house, he opens my door even though we're in his mom's car and not his dad's that has the jammed door.

When I walk past him, he catches my hand. He doesn't have to yank or pull, I come right back to him with ease, letting him hold my hand and shivering even though the night air is crisp and slightly warm. It's my favorite kind of night, starry sky, no clouds, and a big bright moon. JJ leans against the car and we both gaze at the sky. Unlike me, he knows the constellations. I find the whole star mapping thing confusing but the sky sure is beautiful.

"Amazing how one sky can showcase so many things, right?" he says.

"Yeah."

"It is also amazing that you think I hadn't heard that song before."

I begin to smile and bring my head back down. I have so many mixed emotions that I don't know what to do.

"So you know then," I say.

"What do I know?"

"How I think I feel about you."

He lets go of my hand and my heart feels like it's beating inside of my throat. JJ runs his hands through his hair.

"You *think* or you *know*?" he asks.

This question is tougher than it seems and my answer doesn't come right away like I think it should.

JJ does a half smile and then nods slowly. "I have a confession to make," he says, standing up straight.

In my mind I'm hoping he'll say three little words.

"You have been so lost these past couple of months. So many people were impacted by your mom's death that I could only imagine how you must have felt. You're my best friend so my goal was to—"

"Goal?" I interrupt.

"You didn't let me finish. I wanted to help you get back to you. Get back to God and stop hating him so much, because He didn't do this. You know that right? He didn't take your mom away."

I sigh. I know that *now*. I'd learned to stop blaming God for the accident. It was Almond's mom who was at fault. My dad had reminded me to hate the sin, not the sinner.

"What do you mean by *goal*? Was I some kind of project for you?"

"Not at all. I was trying to help you push past your pain because that's what friends do for each other."

It feels like at times we've been more than friends but his whole speech isn't helping. I'm more confused than I was before. I rub my forehead. "JJ, what are you saying?"

"I'm saying that…" He pauses to crack his knuckles.

His delay is giving me anxiety so I rephrase my question. "What exactly do you mean?"

He looks at the ground. "I think we should remain friends. This isn't the right time for us to be more than that. You're still grieving. I mean, you're going to always grieve, but right now, I think it would be very unfair of me to want a relationship with you when you're not whole."

"You think I'm broken?" I'm getting angry.

JJ holds up both hands. "Clove, please hear me out. Don't get mad. I'm just saying that right now isn't a good time. You couldn't even answer my first question, which was do you think you know how you feel or do you *know* how you feel. You're not ready."

"Don't tell me what I'm ready for!"

JJ reaches out for me again, but I yank away. "Don't touch me! You're confusing me!"

Hurt spreads across his face. I'm somewhat contrite because I shouldn't have yelled at him but there are so many questions I need answers to. "Why'd you hold my hand? Why do you look at me the way you do? Why do you keep saying such nice things? Wake up early in the morning to run and spend time with me? Why, huh? Is this a game? Am I a broken puzzle piece you feel like you need to put back together?"

For the umpteenth time this week, my eyes water. I turn away from him.

"Clove, please listen. I—"

"Just go. Leave me alone." Humiliated, I run to the front door.

I'm so frustrated that I can't get the key through the lock fast enough. With blurry vision, I make it inside the house. I lean my back against the door and slide all the way down to the floor. What is wrong with me? One minute I'm all in love and dreaming about kissing JJ. Next, I talk myself out of falling for him. Then when I finally get the chance to say how I feel out loud, I stall. Why?

Everything he said is true. I don't know what I want and I shouldn't say anything until I do know.

## Thirty-Two

# Back to You

Easter Sunday is the day everybody goes to church. People get fancy, dress their kids up in pastel colors, cook duck or some other elaborate dish that they may not normally eat on any other day. Normally, our church is overflowing with people on Easter. Pastor Rob is having four services just to accommodate the crowd he predicts is sure to attend.

Everything about Easter reminds me of how Mama and I would spend time preparing for this day. She'd let Gram straighten my hair and we'd spend hours shopping for the perfect dress and shoes.

This year, I hadn't bothered to shop for a dress. I didn't need one because the yellow-halter dress we bought last year still hangs in my closet with the price tag on it.

Most of my dresses were the long maxi-type, but last year's Easter dress was short and flared at the knees.

"Clove, you have beautiful legs," Mama told me when we were out shopping. "You don't have to hide who you are. Accept it and own it."

Begrudgingly, I took the yellow dress into the fitting room to try on. Perhaps it was the color or the freedom of showing some of my skin but it made me feel as golden as it looked. I absolutely loved it. Mama smiled her biggest smile. "Told ya," she said. "You're stunning, Buttercup! I'm getting this dress for you."

"No Mama! It's too much." We argued a little, but ultimately she won. However, once Sunday came around, I was too self-conscious to even put it on.

The dress rests in my closet. I smooth my hands over it and sigh. I'd told JJ I would be there for him today but I'm still not feeling up to it. A part of me wants to go for a run, but Gram has already straightened my hair, so running would only make it revert back to its natural state. Not to mention, I'm afraid I'll run into JJ.

Over the past few days, I've thought about our dispute. He had to know he was sending me mixed signals. I could've sworn he was feeling what I was feeling. Maybe he's right. The two of us in a relationship might be too much.

With the need to clear my mind. I put on something comfortable to walk in and quietly leave out of the front door.

I scroll through the playlist JJ sent me and notice that he's added another song. As I listen to it, I monitor the sky. It's overcast so I may not be able to see the sunrise. I put my hands into the front pocket of my sweatshirt and play the songs on JJ's list.

When I reach the hill, I stare at it for a while. I hadn't tried to climb up here without JJ's help but today it's just me. If I want to go up, I'll have to do it on my own.

Once I reach the top, I look at the tree, hoping JJ would be there leaning against it. He's not. However, the tree that I thought was dead has leaves growing on its once bare twigs. Guess it just needed more time.

Closing my eyes, I let the sounds and smells of the morning consume me. I feel the breeze blow through my hair. The birds chirp, cheering on the arrival of day. Although it's cloudy, the sky is bright because even the clouds can't hold back the sun's shine.

I get a sense that someone is behind me. Turning around, I see JJ going back down the hill.

"JJ, wait! Please don't leave."

He stops in his tracks but doesn't face me. "I'm sorry, I didn't know you'd be here."

"You don't have to leave."

"You told me to leave you alone. I don't want to bother you."

"You're not bothering me. Please come, sit." I pat the space beside me.

After he sits I notice that he's not sweating. "Did you walk here instead of running?"

"Yes."

"Really? Thought you loved running."

He shrugs. "Lately, I've just felt like slowing down a bit."

I run my fingers through the grass. Slowing down to think about things would have been good for me as well. "JJ, I'm so sorry for the things I said and for yelling at you. You were right about us just being friends. I wasn't thinking clearly and….and…" I can't think of what else to say.

"You think I was right?" he asks.

The fact that he's asking makes me pause and question myself. But ultimately, I do think he was right. "Yes," I say. "I have things I still need to sort through and I value our friendship too much to prematurely jump into something more especially knowing that I might be moving."

JJ nods slowly then puts his hand around the back of his neck. "I should apologize to you too. I never meant to hurt you. That wasn't my intention."

"What was your intention?"

He shakes his head. "I don't know. I mean, I know but maybe it won't come out right."

"Try me."

JJ pulls up blades of grass and lets them fall back down to the earth. "Remember when my mom had a miscarriage right after my granddad passed away?"

I do remember. Caleb was still a baby and Mr. Jourdan was working long hours in Memphis. His mom had just lost both her parents as well, and she was struggling to be present with her family. JJ was thirteen and doing his best to help his mom by taking care of his siblings. He made his first B ever on a class assignment.

"Yeah," I say. "I remember."

"You and your mom came over every day for like a month, maybe more. You two baked, cooked, and even cleaned for us. With my dad going back and forth to work in Memphis every day, I was coming home from school trying to take care of everyone until Dad could get home. We weren't poor, but with mom out of commission, I was struggling to do everything. It was like you and Miss Honey were angels in our lives; an answered prayer," JJ continues. "The kindness and generosity you two showed was just what my mom needed. It's what we all needed, just a little help for a little while."

The wind blows his hair into his face, but he doesn't move it out of the way. I can tell he's thinking back to that time and I think about it too. We've been friends through many of life's ups and downs. All of it has made us stronger. I take JJ's hand and gently squeeze it. Not for any romantic reason, or because there's butterflies in my stomach, but as a way to tell him I understand and I appreciate him.

Out of the corner of my eye, I see something flutter. A butterfly flies right in front of us, landing on the grass. It's odd because butterflies land near flowers, not people or just plain grass. But it stays there, showcasing its gorgeous, orange wings, opening and closing them for us to admire.

"You think it's waiting on us to give it a message?" I whisper to JJ. Saying I love you to a butterfly so it can take that message to heaven still sounds funny to me, but this butterfly seems like it's waiting for us to whisper to it.

"You go first," he says.

"What do I say?"

He shrugs. "Whatever message you want it to send."

JJ told me if you whisper *I love you* it would take the message to heaven. "I love you," I say to the butterfly. "Your turn, JJ."

He waits a few seconds. "I love you too," he says.

The butterfly flies high into the sky as if it might actually take our message to heaven. When I look at JJ again, our eyes meet. I think about what he said: *I love you too.* Was he talking to me or the butterfly?

"I should get back home," he says, breaking our gaze. "I have to sing for three services today."

I chuckle. "Stop playing. You can't sing. This is just a hoax to get me to come to church."

He stands and gives me his hand to lift me up. "Only one way to find out. Would you mind if I walk you home?"

I look at my watch. "Maybe we should run, it's getting close to service time. Race you to the stop sign?"

"Race? As in, you think you can beat me?"

I smile. "I don't think, I *know*."

He chuckles. "This I gotta see."

Ready to run, I prepare my stance. "On your mark…get set…"

I take off running and then yell, "Go!"

# Epilogue

Where am I? My heart beats so fast that I think it's going to burst out of my chest. Rising to my feet, I survey the area. I'm downtown. *Kate's Cakes and Coffee* is to the right of me. The Government building is to the left. Aromas of fresh bread and pastries draw me into the bakery where the bell chimes as soon as I walk in.

"Be right with you," a voice calls from the back. What is going on? I hadn't been here since January. Nothing's changed. Everything's still the same. The signs, the punny posters like *Donut forget a napkin, They see Me Rollin*-with a picture of a rolling pin, *All this sugar, got me hooked*-with a mixer and hook attached; they're all still hanging on the wall. I used to think these posters were funny. It's making me smile even though this whole scene is perplexing.

I gasp as the woman who greeted me wipes her hands on a towel in the back. Her apron is tied around her petite frame. Her hair is pulled into a low bun and covered with a hair net. I can almost smell her scent of cinnamon, vanilla, and clove from here.

"Good morning, Buttercup! What can I get you?"

I can't talk. I really can't form words because I think I'm dreaming—I *should* be dreaming but everything feels so real. I reach out to touch her and meet flesh, warm flesh. This doesn't make any sense. Am I dead?

She comes from behind the counter and swallows me into the tightest hug that only she can give.

Tears fill my eyes.

"Don't you cry now, sweetie. I am very happy here. The pay is good, the hours aren't long, I'm doing what I love and I get to sleep in a really big mansion. Would you like to see it?"

Around us there are a few customers sitting down, reading newspapers or tablets, and sipping mugs steaming with hot liquid. Are we just gonna leave the customers in here?

Mama smiles as if she's read my thoughts. "They'll be fine. Come with me."

She takes my hand, leading me back outside where the front bakery sign says *Honey's Sweets*.

I'm finally able to speak. "Mama, is this your bakery?"

Mama grins. "Yes! You like it?"

"I love it!"

Underneath my feet are gold bricks. Not yellow-gold, but real gold. Downtown looks brand new, bright, and beautiful. It's like seeing the *Wizard of OZ* in full HD but far better.

In the blink of an eye I see a mansion that's so big, I can't take it all in. It's surrounded by gates made of pearl and there are people guarding it.

The gates open and Mama points. "My home is in there. I was waiting at the shop for you," she tells me. Her brilliant white smile reaches her eyes as she gently grabs my chin. "I'm so glad you came back," she whispers.

I don't know what she means by "back." I've never been here before. I thought I had, but I hadn't. Everything here is almost indescribable.

"You've come back to your first love," she says. "In life, the road gets messy and the journey has twists and turns. You will stumble, you will trip, you may fall, but always remember to come back. To get back up and stay the course. Alright Buttercup?"

I understand so I nod. An orange butterfly, identical to the one JJ and I saw, lands on her shoulder.

Mama smiles. "I got your message. You know that I love you always. I have to go now and so do you." She begins to float away.

"Mama, wait," I call after her. There are so many things I need to say, so many questions I want to ask. "Clove, I will always be with you," her voice becomes a whisper. She blows me a kiss and I blow one back. The vision before me starts to blur and fade.

In the blink of an eye, I'm back in my room. My alarm clock reads 9:00 a.m.

I'm in shock. Finally, I've had a dream about Mama and I haven't woken up at 5 a.m. The sleep, the dream, the way I feel, it's all good. Mama's all good. There's this peacefulness I feel that I just can't seem to explain. Smiling to myself, I reach for my phone.

**Me:** *Good morning! How's Science Camp so far?*

JJ is probably busy with his campers, but maybe he'll have a break to reply back. I wait for a few seconds.

**JJ:** *Hey!!! Good Morning! Science camp is good. Kind of crazy, but good. How's ATL w/ ur Aunt Didi?*

**Me:** *It's cool. Guess what?*

**JJ:** *What?*

**Me:** *I finally had a dream about my mom. She was in heaven, owned her own bakery and everything. I swear I saw and felt her like it was the real thing.*

**JJ:** *That's amahsome! I'm glad you were able to see her!*

**Me:** *Amahsome???*

**JJ:** *Amazing and awesome. These kids got me combining words*

**Me:** *LOL! Crazy thing, that butterfly we whispered to was there on her shoulder. Weird right?*

**JJ:** *Not weird, I think that's beautiful.*

He's right, the dream was beautiful. I want to tell him more but I also want to tell him that I miss him, even though we're only a week into our summer vacay. Friends tell each other they miss each other, right?

**Me:** *I miss you.*

We agreed to be friends, but sometimes JJ says and does things that make me think we'd be great at being more than friends.

**JJ:** *I miss you two*

**JJ:** **too. Can we talk later? We're getting ready for a hike.*

**Me:** *Of course. Text me anytime.*

**JJ:** *Um no. I meant TALK-talk. Not text. I miss hearing your voice.*

See. Things like that put flutters inside my stomach. He always knows when to say the right things. I think about sending him a blushing emoji, but instead I choose something different: a butterfly emoticon.

**Me:** *})i(}*

I put my phone down and get out of bed, but then it vibrates.

**JJ:** *})i(}, })i(}*

*See what happens next!*

JJ and Clove's journey is far from over. Check out the rest of the Loved by You series.

Book 2, The Strawberry Pact

Book 3, It Never Rains in Las Vegas

<h1 style="text-align:center">Mama's Ginger Molasses Cookies</h1>

By Gwenda Anthony

¾ cup of shortening

1 cup sugar

2 Tablespoons of blackstrap molasses

2 Tablespoons of maple syrup

1 egg

2 cups of flour

½ teaspoon of cinnamon

½ teaspoon of cloves

½ teaspoon of ginger

½ teaspoon of salt

2 teaspoons of baking soda

1 teaspoon ground ginger

2 large eggs

3 1/2 cups all purpose

Extra sugar for dusting

Sift flour and measure. Add cinnamon, cloves, ginger, salt, and soda. Sift again.  Cream shortening and sugar.  Add egg and mix thoroughly.  Add molasses and syrup and mix well. Stir in flour mixture. Chill thoroughly. Roll dough into small balls in palm of hand.  Roll in granulated sugar and place on greased cookie sheets.  Bake 10 to 12 minutes at 375 F. As these bake, they flatten to form perfect rounds, so please place about 2 inches apart on cookie sheets. Makes 4 to 5 dozen.

# JJ's Sunrise Playlist

*"Clouds"* Trip Lee
*"Sidelines"* Lecrae
*"Pressure"* Andy Mineo
*"Not Today"* Satan KB
*"Til The Day I Die"* Tobymac
*"Real Love"* Hillsong Young and Free
*"Never too Far Gone"* Jordan Feliz
*"Good Feeling"* Austin French
*"In the Water"* Gawvi
*"Can't Live Without"* Hollyn
*"He Said"* Group 1 Crew
*"So Will I (100 Billion X)"* Hillsong United

# Discussion Questions

Please note that some of the questions may contain spoilers if you haven't read the book first.

1. Before this story, had you ever heard of a Golden Birthday?
2. Which character did you like most? Why?
3. Which character was your least favorite? Why?
4. In what ways did Clove's friends help her through a hard time?
5. What do you learn about Clove at the beginning of the story?
6. What does Clove want and why does she think it'll make her happy? What is her misbelief?
7. What themes or truths are displayed through each character?
8. Why do you think Jonah, "JJ", was the one who was able to reach Clove most?
9. Why do you think Jessa was afraid to come out to Clove?
10. What did you think about Clove reaching out to Almond?
11. Did you agree with JJ's decision to postpone dating Clove?
12. Do you think Clove and Jonah will become a couple later?

# Acknowledgments

I did it! I published my first book…for the second time. Lol!

First giving honor to God, who is the head of my life…if you were raised in church you know how the rest of that goes. But for real, I'm a believer and none of this would have been possible without God's guidance.

Second, to my family, thank you for allowing me to take time to write. It means a lot to me. Jamal, thanks for listening, supporting, providing, loving, giving, reaching and growing with me in this walk of life.

To my children, I hope when you're old enough, you read this book. I pray that I've raised to you to be kind-hearted and loving. I want you both to pursue your dreams. You are both fearfully and wonderfully made (Psalms 139:14)

To my dad, thank you for being my biggest promoter. I know mom would be proud and doing the same. Love you! My Aunts and Uncles, GG, Deborah, Mary, Eric, Stephanie, Candace, Devlon, thank you for loving and supporting me.

Christin U, thank you for encouraging me and being my first beta reader. You've been a huge help. Darcel C. thank you for the last minute comb-through and for being a listening ear, encourager and Polo buddy.

To my besties all the way back to Pre-K and beyond: Erin M. and Courtney H. thanks for always being there and supporting my work. Both of you lead busy lives but you make time for me whenever I need you.

Miya Rene, you rock! You're always so supportive of me and always give a listening ear. Melanie, totally miss you, but I'm glad we still keep in touch and can chat until one of our kids distract us. Cheryl, Rosie, Shelena-CB4! Y'all are my Las Vegas sisters for life! Ms. Latrina M. thank you for your on going support. To my book club friends, I enjoy our time together learning about new books. It's always a slice!

Margo, I appreciate your initial edits when Back to You was just beginning. Your edits and support have been super helpful.

To everyone who has supported me in my journey, THANK YOU, THANK YOU, THANK YOU!

# About the Author

K. Anthony Wilson also affectionately known as "Kat", is a girl raised in the south. From Tennessee, she moved to Las Vegas for college and for new adventure. And what an adventure it was! Oh the stories she could tell…and she probably will.

She enjoys adventures with her two children, who love exploring the outdoors. When she's not hiking, exploring, baking, cleaning, cooking, crocheting, reading, and writing; she's looking for a time to take a nap.

*Back to You* is the first in a previous series titled *Loved by You*. There are more books to come so stay tuned!

**You can connect with me on:**

🌐 https://k-anthonywilson.com